The Dressmaker's Daughter

by Linda Boroff

SANTA
MONICA
PRESS
TEEN

Published by: Santa Monica Press LLC
P.O. Box 850
Solana Beach, CA 92075
1-800-784-9553
www.santamonicapress.com
books@santamonicapress.com

Printed in the United States

ISBN-13 978-1-59580-107-4 (print)
ISBN-13 978-1-59580-783-0 (ebook)

Publisher's Cataloging-in-Publication data

Names: Boroff, Linda, author.
Title: The dressmaker's daughter / by Linda Boroff.
Description: Solana Beach, CA: Santa Monica Press, 2022.
Identifiers: ISBN: 978-1-59580-107-4 (print) | 978-1-59580-783-0 (ebook)
Subjects: LCSH Jews--Persecutions--Romania--History--Fiction. | Holocaust, Jewish (1939-1945)--Romania--Fiction. | Jews--Romania--History--20th century--Fiction. | Historical fiction. | Romance fiction. | BISAC YOUNG ADULT FICTION / Historical / Holocaust | YOUNG ADULT FICTION / Romance / Historical | YOUNG ADULT FICTION / War & Military | YOUNG ADULT FICTION / Religious / Jewish
Classification: LCC PS3602.O7662 D74 2022 | DDC 813.6--dc23

Cover and interior design and production by Future Studio

Pages 203-204: "Hymn of the Partisans," written by Hirsh Glick, a young Jewish poet, partisan, and inmate of the Vilna Ghetto.

Cover and interior design and production by Future Studio
Cover art: iStock.com/ChiccoDodiFC, iStock.com/Alesikka

Contents

Spring 1944, Somewhere Outside Bershad

WE RISE AND GET GOING as soon as the last faint glow of the sunset disappears and night glides in to reclaim the forest. All day I have watched the sky impatiently, admonishing myself for wishing away what could be my last hours on earth. I have already checked my gun and ammunition countless times; I have my instructions, my part in the action, memorized and imprinted like a brand on my memory, but I go over everything yet again as I wait.

My ears, sensitized to the slightest sound, now bring in the quietly whispered Hebrew prayers of one of the partisans, probably Jonah. Raised by a passionately atheist father, I have comparatively little knowledge of the Jewish religion, and the sonorous murmuring of the various chants had once been a meaningless jumble of syllables to me. But now I am able to make out certain phrases and know what they mean. I even speak them sometimes, for what it is worth.

We have been waiting restlessly all day, whiling away the hours with our own thoughts, searching for any unlikely hint of rain, which would cause postponement of the action. Instead, the day had dawned brilliant and remained clear and fresh. The whole forest announces and welcomes spring with tender, pale green new growth, the atmosphere as still and clean as though the worst war ever perpetrated by man has not been raging around and through it for years now. I see the wildflowers reaching up their hopeful, tentative buds, although the chaos of battle could arrive anytime to rip apart and bury them before they could bloom, summon the bees, and pollinate for the next generation.

They are like us in their unquenchable hope. We, too, risk never reaching the potential that nature intended for us, but still we awaken and offer our faces and vision to the skies every morning.

Now, as night deepens, Jonah has lapsed into his usual silence before an action; I have become used to his taciturnity and leave him undisturbed. I know that he, too, is going over and over the logistics of the attack, making sure that every detail, every potential hitch has been addressed. I can't resist stealing looks, though, at his tense, lanky form, reclining against the bare trunk of a dead elm tree. For the hundredth time I wish for a sketchbook—and the artistic talent to use it to record these moments for . . . for what? I ask myself. For posterity and immortality? The overwhelming odds are that my artwork would wind up disintegrating in the mud of a shell hole.

Our chances of emerging alive from this attack on the German supply lines are not even worth calculating. If we live, we live. If we die, we die. We all know that death can come in a flash and erase all of our ambitions and dreams, our hopes and histories. Worse, we could be captured and endure a fate far worse than death at the hands of our enemies. We are all each other's archives, so that if one survives the war, we can tell the world who our comrades have been: their names, their families, and what they have us memorize about them if they no longer have a voice.

Georgi now walks into the center of the clearing and gives the terse, economical nod to all that is our signal to move. Jonah glances at last in my direction, and I, too, nod slightly, which is all the recognition of our relationship that he will allow in front of the others. But that fleeting eye contact is enough to exchange all of our feelings for one another. It is more than enough.

A surge of renewal and strength courses through my mind and body—so changed from just two years ago. I had been an indulged and pampered daughter of fifteen, dressing and styling and painting myself even as the Nazi shadow spread across Europe.

I look at my hands, strong and skilled, trained now both to heal and to kill. And my muscular arms, tanned and scarred here and there, with each mark telling a story. What would the Daniela of 1941 have thought of this body? I don't dwell on the rest of the changes that now reside within; the brutality that has been inflicted on me, leaving comparatively little mark on the outside but proving my strength and resilience. I am grateful that Mihail had been my first lover. What others I have known—Jonah, the major, and of course the outrages that brutal Romanian and German soldiers have wrought on me—don't matter. They have passed through me like the wind passes through the forest. Of them all, only Mihail remains; he alone is in my heart.

We stand in a small circle, the twelve of us, and touch

fists in the center before breaking apart and melting into the forest. Our destination is a stretch of railroad tracks just outside Bershad that we intend to disable. And if we can take out any Nazi soldiers in the course of the action, that would be a bonus. At the thought, my hand reflexively checks my gun yet again. I am ready.

Come, Return with Me

I WAS BORN Daniela Mielstone in Yedinitz, a town that sat on the border of two troubled nations: Russia and Romania. Over the decades, we had been yanked back and forth between them like a piece of taffy—or I should say a torn piece of bleeding flesh between two predators.

My family was not rich, but my mother was a talented seamstress who made fashionable clothes for wealthy Jews and gentiles alike. Her customers came from as far away as Kishinev, the capital of Bessarabia, sometimes waiting months for a fitting. It was said that Mama could create curves on a woman where none existed, or make excess flesh disappear like magic. She supported our family almost entirely, but we never prospered because, being Jewish, she did not dare to charge anywhere near the value of what her work was worth.

My father had once been ordained as an Orthodox rabbi, but he became an atheist and a socialist before I was born. An easygoing, humorous man, he often hung around the tavern, drinking and telling ribald, impious jokes. Any religious observance in our family, denied nurturing and recognition, had atrophied and faded away, fueling gossip in our town year after year, holiday after holiday. If not for my mother, who was universally respected, we would have been a scandal.

As a child, I was brilliant, a prodigy, but for a woman during these times, that was a misfortune. It made me curious about forbidden things and caused me to push back against tradition and embarrass my family.

Large, strong hands; long, sturdy legs. My dark eyebrows slanted rather exotically—diabolically, some hinted—above greenish eyes shadowed and ringed by nature, not artifice. People told me I looked "Oriental." In our small bookstores, I had glimpsed the covers of pornographic novels from Warsaw and St. Petersburg. I imagined some lustful Mongol warrior, sword aloft, ravishing some remote ancestor of mine during a long-forgotten battle. And his sensual nature had lurked in our heritage for generations, to finally emerge and fill me with forbidden fantasies and desires, eclipsing the pious, disciplined Jewish forebears who rather should have shaped me.

By age fifteen, I had grown from a clever, impetuous child into a tempest. I was hopeless with the needle, forcing my mother to hire village girls and teach them the complex, tiny stitches, each perfect and alike as the one before. I lived only for books. They were my escape, my religion. There was nothing I would not read, even *Mein Kampf*, passed to me clandestinely by a man I had met in the bookstore, a Communist. Had I been caught with it I would have been sent to the madhouse.

But some people believed I was already half mad. My intelligence, blocked at every turn by the suffocating environment of a traditional *shtetl*, took its outlet in explosive tantrums. "If I used such language to my family," said the housewife next door, "I would not see the sun rise."

Sometimes when I was ranting and sobbing, I would feel a great surge of demonic energy, like a racehorse escaping from the starting gate. I was oblivious to decorum, blind to consequences. I heard that some people feared me. And I feared myself. What if madness spilled from my brain and coursed through my limbs like a river of fire, claiming my mind entirely? I had seen photos of strait-jacketed people in bleak madhouses; and we knew that Hitler was executing the mentally ill, even children. I knew that Romania was trying to emulate his crimes, especially toward the Jews.

My dark, wavy hair plunged to my waist, escaping even the sternest bindings and braids. I was tall for my age and willowy, but strong like a mare. My dream was to be a doctor, surely not the ideal vocation for such a rebel. But I craved the power to battle death and illness, even with our primitive, ineffectual medicines. I imagined myself working in a large hospital in Warsaw or Vilna or even New York. I would teach myself chemistry, pathology, discover new remedies, cure cancer!

The Romanians, always anti-Semitic, had recently intensified their oppression, closing down religious schools and barring most Jews from the gymnasium, the local high school. But if I learned basic science and mathematics, I could apply to a university far from home. So my weary, long-suffering parents gave in at last and engaged me a tutor.

This is where my story really begins.

My Senses Awaken

DO YOU BELIEVE in love at first sight? Some movies portray love as a cyclone wrenching one's soul from its foundation. But for me, love was a sunrise. From the fierce night of my rebellious isolation, a light glowed, and soon the horizon was aflame. The sky changed hue a million times.

He was eighteen, and I fifteen, and if I were to stop right there, my story would be a scandal. Even the word fifteen sounds salacious. I have seen the faces of respected men—religious leaders, professors ... change subtly at that notion of "fifteen" though they think they are hiding their lust.

But before I tell of my tutoring, I must introduce one more person. Philippa McEnery was the British nanny to the children of our local noble, Count Kányádi. The Count, in his late forties, was a businessman whose grandfather had made a fortune purveying steel to the railroad industry. The count lived in London most of the year, and I had seen him only twice: blond, urbane, and well-dressed. I naturally imagined that he kept mistresses.

The countess considered our town a provincial backwater. When she came here, she patronized my mother—not for evening dress, but for less formal wear. She would say, with a sidelong glance at my father, that my mother had the talent to become a Paris couturier if she would consider moving, but my mother would always demur. She was happy with her life in this village where she had grown up.

Philippa sometimes accompanied the countess when she came for a fitting. She was highly educated by our standards and disheveled in an elegant way. Philippa's British nationality seemed to cast a protective nimbus around her, as if the entire empire stood her guard. She made fun of the Nazis, the Romanian gendarmes, the Russians—and of course her own country, too. Nothing escaped her sly, mischievous wit. Nobody ever chided or hushed her.

One day, while the countess was occupied with my mother, Philippa struck up a conversation with me in the front parlor. I was enchanted with her. She had an exquisite profile, fit for a cameo, and limpid blue eyes that slanted downward slightly at the outer corners, giving her a wistful air. Catlike as a dancer, she sat erect yet relaxed in a way that I tried to emulate. She spoke Russian, German, and Romanian, but was eager to learn Yiddish and full of curiosity about Judaism.

"Tell me about Esther in the Bible," Philippa said. "She was very brave, yes?"

"I am not the person to ask about such things," I said with a laugh. "We're non-observant."

"But the Bible says she saved her nation. Your nation."

"The Bible is a set of fables and exaggerations."

"Blasphemer, quiet down," my mother shouted from the sewing room through a mouthful of pins.

Philippa then asked me, in a lower tone, about circumcision—why the Jews felt the need to ritually alter their sons.

"We don't view it that way," I said to her, trying to appear casual and offhand about men—whom I had absolutely no firsthand knowledge of. "But I can see how one might."

"Some women prefer their men so," Philippa said with a wink. "I don't suppose you have a basis for comparison . . . yet?" My mouth dropped open, but after a moment I smiled back. I knew now that I had a fellow conspirator in whom I could confide absolutely *anything*.

As the Germans intensified their violence, the entire world suffered in a queasy state of apprehension. People tried to reassure themselves that, as bad as things were, at least we here were not at war, but the comfort was hollow.

Portents that foretold the immensity of the evil swarming toward us were everywhere. Sometimes when I slept, a man's voice loud as a thunderclap would shout my name, jolting me awake. In the mornings, the sky weighed upon me like lead and the sun emerged the color of brass. I crossed myself in private and said Catholic prayers, repeating "protective" words or oaths under my breath like a spell. I grew irrationally afraid of the number three. All this was proof of incipient insanity. I would hold my head in my hands and rock back and forth, begging for one more month, one more day, before I went stark mad and dashed through the village naked or murdered a stranger.

Living amidst the violence and uncertainty of my unfortunate country, it's no surprise that I could find no sanctuary from my chaotic thoughts. Our village had been occupied by Romania since World War I ended in 1918. For the Jews, the Romanians' twenty-two-year regime had meant terror, corruption, bribery, suppression, and unpredictable, capricious arrests. To the Romanians, we Jews were the eternal outsiders, though we had lived here for a thousand years. Yet despite the hate and injustice, we muddled through: like all people, we had the stubborn capacity to get on with life, to become accustomed and endure. To survive.

But now in 1940, Europe had erupted into war like a volcano spewing magma. Hitler had taken over Czechoslovakia; he had been welcomed in the streets of Austria by joyous crowds as if he were some wise, heroic liberator rather than a greedy butcher. Now he was dismembering Poland, gorging down her resources, murdering Polish intellectuals and countless others. And of course the worst Nazi cruelty was reserved for the Jews. Now the British stood alone fighting the maniac Hitler, and even they were barely holding him off. Most other countries of Europe now lay in a trance of dread. Maybe, they must have hoped, if they prayed enough, things would somehow come right.

My father couldn't figure out how the world had allowed Hitler to rearm in plain view after the 1914–18 "Great War" as we then called World War I. He had boldly announced his intention to take revenge for Germany's humiliation, while the world stood in confusion and disbelief and did nothing.

But on this day, in these precious, waning days before the storm, Yedinitz was still a picturesque blend of old and new Europe: occasional motorcars shared the unpaved road with donkeys, horses, and goats. Jews and gentiles strolled the narrow sidewalks navigating their way amid street markets and tiny shops.

The earth at least was kind to us. We were flush with orchards—apples, pears, cherries, and plums, ripe and sweet for the eating. Walk a short way outside of town in summer, and you heard vast choruses of birds; beyond the fields, the forest was a shimmering, whispering sea of green, and in the fall it turned to russet and gold. When winter came we would sleigh ride behind horses, speeding through an icy white, moonlit world. We knew that the war was inevitable, but still we clung to our narrowing universe of desperate hope.

Count Kányádi didn't want his hunting parties disrupted by soldiers tramping around, so he pulled strings and distributed bribes, first to the Romanians and then to the Russians, to keep them at a distance. So that was how we had come to live in a bubble, a peaceful fool's paradise in the very teeth of the war that was now blazing across Europe.

Our home was a pretty two-story house just off the main street, surrounded by lush trees and bushes; now, in summer, our yard was a riot of flowers. To own a house of two stories was not common in those days. People may have thought that we put on pretensions or lived beyond our means, but since my mother's dressmaking shop took up so much of the first floor, we had added on until the house fit us, almost as if we had tailored it to ourselves like a suit of clothes.

It was a snug fit, warm and comfortable. We actually had running water and flush toilets in our home, still uncommon here in the mid-20th century. For this blessing we had the Countess Kányádi, my mother's best customer, to thank. Other families had to make do with boards sitting above a hole in the ground, with another board for the feet. This was how people lived then and perhaps still do in many places.

When Hitler and Stalin divided up Europe like a carcass, our town in the region of Bessarabia was given to Russia as a gift, like a bauble. The powerful Soviets swept in and ordered Romania's fascist leader, Antonescu, and his minions to leave Bessarabian soil at once. With no choice, the Romanian civil and military authorities packed up and departed the land they had oppressed since 1918. None of us Jews grieved their departure, you may be sure.

Forgive us—for Stalin was the nadir of wickedness—but from the Russians, the Communists, we Jews dared hope for a bit more freedom and equality. They couldn't treat us worse than the Romanians, we figured. We imagined we were to be rescued by the invincible Red Army. When the soldiers appeared in the street, we actually hugged one another and cried with joy—we had suffered so much under the previous tyranny.

In the Fading Glow of Peace

I CAME HOME one afternoon with my friend Priva, a sweet, unworldly girl from a pious family who nevertheless stuck loyally by me when people shook their heads at my behavior and predicted a "bad outcome."

We had been to the bookstore, and I had invited her for tea. Our home seemed spacious and comfortable to her, compared to her humbler, traditional bungalow. She loved staring at our polished mahogany sideboards displaying family china and heirlooms; our rugs were old but fine. We had candelabra and comfortable armchairs—even a radio that could have kept us informed of the war, but it seemed far away, and Mama tuned in music to keep her seamstresses entertained.

Priva and I hurried through the parlor to my mother's busy workroom. As usual, it was a hive of activity: women industriously working away at treadle-run sewing machines; the two best workers got the new electric machines. Others sat quietly doing hand work, their minds a million miles away, probably preoccupied with love and sex, as mine certainly was.

This morning, the fussy, portly Countess Kányádi herself was in attendance, standing before a three-way mirror in her corset, surveying herself analytically, front and back. She was in her late thirties, literally bursting with rude health from her pampered, well-nourished life. What a contrast with my mother, ten years older and a graying, faded beauty. Mama's worn, graceful hands held tiny scissors that sliced the last thread on a gorgeous dress. Mama rose, shaking it out.

"Here, Your Grace, I made that little change." She expertly draped the dress over the countess; an assistant ran to help button and smooth it. People said my mother's dresses could make a Betty Grable out of a broomstick . . . or turn a tank into a temptress.

And sure enough, the stunning gown floated down gracefully like a bouquet of silken flowers and transformed the stodgy countess into an elegant, sexy matron with abundant cleavage. The whole room cheered as the countess delightedly modeled it, turning this way and that, looking over her shoulder at her own flirtatious face.

"Miriam, you sorceress! He'll be putty in my hands tonight."

Mama laughed modestly. The countess raised the dress to display her hefty thighs in their satin garters with blue flowers embroidered around the tops. The ladies in the room, staring, let out a mild collective gasp. The countess chortled and shook a finger playfully at Mama: "But if I ever hear of you making a dress for his mistress . . ."

All laughed. Mama, a little taken aback, looked quickly at me and Priva, who were goggling like fish. She turned to me, speaking around the pins she seemed to always have protruding from her lips. "What did you girls waste money on now?"

"Oh nothing, Mama. A few books." I turned quickly to Priva, worried that Mama would ask which books. "Let's go show Papa."

We strolled toward the back of the house, leaving the countess primping and examining herself from all angles. Down a hallway papered in sinuous green vines and pale mauve chrysanthemums—Mama loved flowers both indoors and out—we reached a room lined with books, my father's kingdom, where he reigned and reveled in the wisdom of the ages. My Papa, Samuel—Schmuel in Yiddish—sat reading in his comfortable maroon leather chair at a broad oak desk covered with his notes and research. Papa wrote books whose audience was other intellectuals and radical philosophers. But what with the war and the economic chaos of the Depression in America, he had not published in years. He wasn't too concerned about this; he lived in a world of ideas. And of course Mama's shop ensured that we didn't need the sparse payments he got from struggling publishers.

Papa was in his fifties, ten years older than Mama. My little brother Jacob, nine years old, was here, too, practicing the violin; the vigorous motion of his bow made his head of dark, glossy hair swing and sway about. He was a gifted musician, while I had no particular calling for music. I could read notes and stumble through a few tunes on our piano in the parlor, but I didn't have Jacob's spark of genius or his perfect pitch.

My father seemed to be studying a religious book, even *davening* or bobbing as he read, but as you got closer, you could see that he was reading *The Communist Manifesto*. I laughed, and Priva stared with her large, ingenuous blue eyes.

Papa was an idealist and a public activist. He had absorbed the Russian liberalism that existed before the Revolution and the fall of the Czar. His Judaism had been informed with a sense of social justice. When Papa was young, Mama told me, he had learned ancient Hebrew literature, poetry, and philosophy. These subjects were not merely schoolwork to him; he had been totally immersed and devoted to Judaism; people predicted great things for him as a religious leader, perhaps a rabbi of his own congregation.

And then, he was struck by lightning: He learned about the Theory of Relativity, Einstein's stunning discoveries of space-time and how the speed of light defined and controlled the universe, how whole stars and even galaxies had formed from the tiniest parts of atoms. And as if that weren't enough to shake his world—he learned about Communism.

These two powerful concepts changed more than his attitude, Mama would say. They altered his very brain. He was able to comprehend that perhaps the universe itself had no beginning, no creator, after all. And that under Communism, true justice could arrive and flourish here on earth. Who could blame him for falling in love with these new ideas? My father had been a rabbinical scholar, but science and politics now became his religion.

Despite my father's atheism, my little brother Jacob attended the Jewish elementary school, the *cheder*. My mother, usually deferential to Papa, would not hear of raising him to be an atheistic Communist! But when Jacob first began studying, he did not want to be there at all. He and I both cried bitterly at being separated. The teacher even threatened to chain Jacob in the yard with his goats! But Papa took him to school anyway to at least learn Hebrew and Bible verses. There was great poetry in the Bible, Papa admitted, as long as one didn't take the rest of it too seriously.

Soon enough, the Romanian authorities restricted Hebrew education, forcing parents to send their children now to government public schools. All the Hebrew schools became illegal. This harshness extended to the gymnasia or high schools, too; I was a clever student, and I understood what was being stolen from me: my very future.

"So, Priva," Papa addressed my friend with his dancing, teasing brown eyes, "your parents still let you visit this house of heresy?"

Priva smiled shyly. "Mr. Mielstone, don't you even believe in Torah?"

"No, I do not," said my father, his eyes alight with mischief. He had been waiting for this opportunity. "All religion," he said, "is bool-sheet, pardon my language." He often used American slang, thinking it a more honest, forthright way to talk.

Priva looked politely confused at the guttural English words.

"Priests," shouted my father, gathering steam, "rabbis, wizards, magicians. One and the same. All bool-sheeters since time began."

"Papa! Okay, enough!" I tried not to laugh. Once Papa got going, he could rant for an hour about the irrationality and unfairness of capitalism and organized religion. All religions—he didn't care which—were lies. And we Jews were the worst because we called ourselves the pioneers, the originators of monotheistic belief—of one

God—rather than multitudes of gods with each ruling their own separate domain: the sun, the tides, the trees, the underworld.

"And are the Roman and Greek gods any more false than our own version?" Papa would ask. "No! They're all equally false. A lie is a lie. Isn't it enough we're bullied by the *goyim*?" He cried out nearly pounding the table. "Now I should grovel to some 'ruler of the universe,' too? What has your God done for us Jews lately?" He pointedly asked Priva, who had pasted a quavering smile onto her face. "Hah! You have no answer! The answer is *nichts*. Nothing. Nothing does nothing."

"Papa, *genug*!" I laughed. "Enough!" I was bold with him because we were cut from the same cloth, rebels through and through. But I also watched Priva nervously from the corner of my eye. Her family was respectable and conservative; what if they banned her from visiting this house—or worse, from even being my friend?

"So! What mischief have you girls been up to?"

"We've been to the bookshop, Papa," I said boldly.

"Ha! The most dangerous place in town! Show me."

We laughingly protested as Papa seized my bag and brought out a couple of seamy, popular romance novels. On the covers, full-lipped beauties in gaudy satin and lace displayed their cleavages to nobles with long hair and enormously bulging codpieces. Jacob abruptly left his violin to peek at the pages. Papa reached into the bag and drew out Emma Goldman's autobiography.

"Emma Goldman, the American anarchist. Well chosen! She had the courage of her beliefs. But she also lived long enough to see her dearest theories land in the trash heap of history."

I glanced at Papa's *Communist Manifesto* and almost asked if his own precious book might not someday land there, too, but thought better of it.

"And now," said Papa, "a greater evil than capitalism is stalking us." He motioned at a newspaper featuring the glaring scowl of Adolf Hitler. "Yes, the worst person ever born. And the Romanian leaders couldn't wait to nuzzle up to the monster's *tuchus.*"

"Papa!"

"Go on. Go read your trash." Papa crinkled his eyes at me understandingly. He and I communicated perfectly with looks and shrugs. Somehow, I knew exactly what he meant, and he could seemingly almost read my mind, too.

Priva and I giggled. We grabbed the bag of books, and Papa returned to his studies as Jacob picked up his violin. We had been a welcome distraction.

In my bedroom, Priva and I sprawled across my bed and tore into our loot. After a few moments, she rolled over and spoke expansively, romantically, to the ceiling.

"Daniela, I want to be Lady Brett Ashley in *The Sun Also Rises.*"

"You and everyone else."

"I want to have affairs with handsome young matadors . . . and drink myself silly all the time. Doesn't that sound splendid?"

With a conspiratorial grin, I reached under my bed and drew out *Lady Chatterley's Lover.* Priva gasped, afraid to even touch the book, as if it would burn her. She knew it was banned because of the explicit sex scenes. I opened the book to a well-marked spot, and we both bent over the pages. After a moment, Priva covered her mouth.

Then she let out a little scream and laughed, hiding her face.

"I don't believe it! People really do that?"

"Shhhhh! You'll get me in trouble, you infant!" I playfully pulled Priva's hair.

She pulled mine back. My hair is so thick it was much easier for her to get a good handful than it was for me to pull her ginger tresses that fell through my hand like the silken threads Mama kept for embroidery.

"Do people really put flowers in their hair . . . down there?"

"Why not? If they're in love."

"Daniela, it's so wanton."

"Wanton is good. If you feel love, then there's no holding back. Do you understand?"

"I . . . think so."

"Then there's hope for you!"

"But none for *you*, you bad girl." Priva pulled my hair again. She left with *Lady Chatterley's Lover* tucked deep into her bag of books.

Downstairs, Mama was bidding goodbye to a rich, fussy client. She gave me a meaningful look, and when we were alone, she turned to me.

"Daniela, you could be a little friendlier to my patrons. They pay our bills."

"Oh, Mama," I said lightly, "you're friendly enough for the both of us."

But Mama would not be put off. She was truly angry at me for some reason. "And your skirt is way too short! It's rolled up at the waist. I see what you did. This isn't Hollywood, Daniela. You have your reputation to consider. What's wrong with you?"

"Who cares about Hollywood? Mama, I've decided to become a doctor!"

From his room, Papa heard and shouted out, "At last! A beam of light pierces the darkness."

My mother surveyed me with infinite skepticism. "And which novel inspired this worthy ambition? Or which actress? Ingrid Bergman? Vivien Leigh?"

I was a little hurt that she considered me such a shallow creature. "No, Mama, I've decided on my own."

"And how, tell me, is a Jewish girl supposed to get into medical school? They don't even let Jews into grammar school anymore."

My face fell at this response, and Mama put an arm around me. "Let's be realistic, darling. If you would show even a little interest in dress design—"

"You just said you don't want me to waste my brains on frivolous fashion."

My mother winced. "No, it's better to stay in your room reading pornography!"

"It's literature!"

"Yes, of course. *Literature.*"

I'd had enough of this pecking. Mama was tired, and she was taking it out on me. Offended, I turned away and ran up the stairs as Mama sank into a chair.

"She's young, Mir, full of ideas," I heard Papa saying. I lingered on the steps to eavesdrop. "She's stifled. She needs a goal. Something big enough to occupy that brain of hers. Why not medicine? It's a practical dream."

Mama smiled at the oxymoron. "And while she dreams away, I have to hire girls to sew for me. She could at least learn to operate a machine. Or do the buttonholes. It's you who puts those ideas in her head. A doctor! Instead of telling her to help me out. You do me no favors."

"I'm afraid you have two useless dreamers on your hands then," said Papa.

Jacob skipped into the living room. "Three! I'm hopeless, too!"

"No, darling, you have a true gift." I saw Mama beaming indulgently at her favorite, but I wasn't resentful. Jacob could not help being born to charm, while I was born to annoy and rebel and provoke.

"Just wait," Jacob was saying, "I'll make lots of money on the concert stage, and I'll give it all to you." Mama hugged him.

I went back into my room and withdrew *Mein Kampf* from behind my bookshelf—the evilest book in the world. Is it wrong to know one's enemy? I wanted to know what Hitler was saying to the masses to make them hate us so much. But if I were caught with this particular book, I could not even imagine the punishment. I flopped on the bed and read intently—it was irrational, poorly written, a boring, tedious, screed of hate and lies: just what I had expected.

It grew late, and after what I had read, I could not sleep. All my pleasure and innocence seemed to have been leached from me and replaced with fear. I wandered downstairs through the quiet house, everything set up so neatly for the day tomorrow.

Quietly, I slipped outside into the chilly, windy yard under a moon that passed through the clouds as if spying and peeking at me. I began to whirl and turn under the moon's mystical light, imagining myself at an exotic ball. Moments later, I felt the first droplets of rain on my flushed, feverish skin. Soon a downpour was hammering me, soaking my night clothes, which drew the heat from my body like a wick. I lifted my burning face and drank the fresh rainwater.

My old fear of going mad returned. I crossed myself and said a Hail Mary, just to see what would happen. I was now completely drenched, my teeth chattering like castanets. Quietly, dripping water, I reentered through the kitchen door and stole upstairs. Everything was still, quiet, and serene.

I ran into my room and slipped on the hardwood floor, landing with a thud.

"Daniela, are you all right?"

"Yes. Leave me alone!" I shouted back.

But Mama climbed out of bed and entered my room tentatively. Her face crumpled with worry and shock when she saw me sitting on the floor in a puddle.

"Mama," I said, rising, "what made you become a dressmaker?"

"Just get out of those wet clothes. I'll tell you whatever you want to know." Teeth still chattering, I changed into a nightdress in my closet. "My father was a tailor, as you know," said my mother. "So it was only natural—" But suddenly she stopped herself. "No, that's not it."

She sat beside me now on the bed and stroked my wet hair and face.

"Tell me, Mama."

"When I was a girl, I sensed that people didn't like me very much."

"You? That's ridiculous. People adore you!"

"Perhaps now, some are fond of me. But when I was young, I always felt . . . unlovable."

"That's just how I feel!"

"I thought if I could learn to please people with my sewing, then they would accept me. And it's worked!" She paused, looking at me keenly. "Your father and I have decided to help you become a doctor, if that's really what you want."

I bounced upward on the bed as if a huge weight had been lifted from my shoulders. "Oh, Mama!" I cried, "to be a doctor! It's everything!" I leaped onto the floor and jumped over and over for joy.

"It's your father's notion, really. He wants to get you a tutor, since your mathematics and chemistry will have to be greatly improved if you want to go to medical school. You can study here at home, pass the entrance exams, and perhaps go to London. Or even America. Why not? We have saved for our children. If Jacob can go to a music conservatory, then you can become a doctor if that's what you want. Now try to get some sleep, and we'll talk in the morning." She hugged me and tucked me in.

When the door closed, I sprang from my bed and paced like a tiger, full of excitement. I craved the power to heal, to battle death and relieve suffering! I would find new therapies, medical breakthroughs, cure cancer! My fear of madness left me.

I looked at myself in the mirror and leaned close, studying my face as if seeing the promise of the future there. Little did I know then that God sometimes takes away one madness . . . only to send another.

Dancing at the Precipice

"DANIELA," said my father to me a few days later, "we have found you a tutor! He can help you catch up and prepare for your exams."

"Oh, Papa! Thank you!" I cried. "You are keeping your promise."

"He'll teach you the basics: algebra, physics."

"I'll work so hard!" I danced and spun again. "You'll never be sorry!"

"I knew his father," said Papa. "A fine teacher. Fired from the gymnasium for being Jewish, of course. So he schooled his children at home. The boy Mihail is supposed to be brilliant. And he can use a little extra money."

Later that afternoon, the countess returned, fuming this time. Her new dress, a perfect fit only last week, had already grown tight in the hips. With her was the pretty, blonde governess Philippa, who had brought the two children, Anton, eight, and Katerina, four, now playing cat's cradle at Philippa's feet.

Fashionably dressed, Philippa sat with her bored, feline poise, half listening to the banter flowing around her about fabrics and measurements, her eyes half closed.

Intrigued, I lingered nearby, staring at Philippa with

admiration. She wore her clothes with an offhand grace that made them look even more flattering.

"I don't know how I put on that weight. I've been starving myself," the countess was complaining. She turned to Philippa. "Tell Miriam how I push my plate away half full! I eat a nibble here, a nibble there. Nothing!"

Philippa nodded obediently, but with a touch of knowing irony.

"I'll just let out the seams a tiny bit," said my mother, "that's all it needs. Nobody will notice a thing."

"A pity we can't all be as skinny as our little governess here," the countess said, gesturing to Philippa. "Don't people ever eat back in England?"

"Not really," Philippa said with a little smile. "They insist on boiling everything until it has the consistency of algae." She made a face.

Still fussing at her ample figure, the countess paused. "Maybe we should try English food on me." Everyone laughed obediently.

Studying Philippa, I looked down at my own plain gray dress with its round white collar and long, modest sleeves. As a Jewess, I must not dress too fashionably or immodestly. That would be putting on airs and attract even greater hatred and envy. I wore the simplest clothes, although if you looked closely you would see that my mother had tailored them exquisitely. It was her way of rebelling. The haters might deny me fashion, but the quality of my clothes would always be beyond their reach. It was Mama's way of defying the Romanian bigots in ways that they were too coarse and ignorant to notice.

I touched my dark, disobedient hair that poured across my shoulders. In contrast, Philippa's honey-colored blonde hair was sleek and perfectly smooth in its up-swept, effortlessly sophisticated style. Sometimes she would wear it down, like the American actress Veronica Lake, and it cascaded across her shoulders and bosom like a wavy golden sea.

The Count and Countess Kányádi lived most of the year in London. But the countess often came to my mother for her clothes. She had even offered to bring us to England with her one year. How I wish we had gone, but her husband the count didn't want to arouse suspicion by trailing so many foreigners in his wake. He feared that my father's Communist politics had made him notorious and unwanted in Britain, even though he respected my father's learning.

Count Kányádi was the definition of urbane—impeccably groomed and dressed. He bought his own tailored suits at Savile Row in London; his shoes were of the finest Spanish or Italian leather; they hardly ever touched our muddy, dusty Yedinitz streets.

But the count was a popular man despite his riches and pretensions, because he was generous to the peasants and business owners. He made a point of patronizing local shops and was always accessible to the minor landlords and administrators who kept things running in his absence. He didn't employ a Jewish overseer like many minor nobles did, because the resentment it aroused among the gentiles would rebound against those he was trying to help.

He would have benefited financially from a scrupulous and honest Jewish overseer, of course. But instead the count indulged and tolerated his overseer, a peasant named Roky, because of his pretty young wife. Everybody knew what was going on between them, including Roky, but the overseer took what he called a "modern" attitude and looked the other way when his wife, Madelina, went to help in the kitchen or "tidy up" at the count's estate.

The countess herself came from a proletarian background, although she had fictionalized an aristocratic ancestry for her own family, even having a coat of arms designed in London for her family with griffins and crossed swords in "gules"—the red heraldic color on many royal insignia.

The countess, whose name was Dumitra, had met the count when she was only thirteen years old, the gossip went, and bewitched him with her sylphlike serpentine wiles and precocious body. Besotted, he had risked his inheritance and married her secretly, and his elderly parents died none the wiser, so Dumitra had become the Countess Kányádi and the matriarch of the count's vast estate.

Over the years, although she lost the burnish of youth, she continued to amuse and charm the count. She had a mischievous irreverence and quick sense of humor, even the ability to laugh at herself, a rare and valuable talent. The count loved the children she gave him, and she was wise enough to indulge him in his extramarital affairs, understanding that bold sensuality was his nature and that fighting it would only bring her to grief. So their marriage was remarkably serene with no shattered illusions or destructive accusations. The countess also grew into a skilled housekeeper who could control Roky's theft without antagonizing him or the other peasants who served the household in their absence.

The count would navigate the town's narrow, rutted

roads, jouncing in his chauffeured touring car from Italy, or he would sometimes drive himself, his kid gloves grasping the gleaming wooden steering wheel—a powerful, polished reminder that a world of incomprehensible variety and luxury existed outside Yedinitz.

The count was calm, confident, and imperious. Born into the ruling class, he didn't bother with the petty morals of the region that he had inherited or the lives of its peasants. But my father interested him; he sometimes visited to debate politics and economics, sitting on the edge of Papa's desk or pacing back and forth in his tweeds and worsteds in Papa's messy room littered with books and journals. He appreciated Papa's intellectual discipline and relished matching wits with somebody as skeptical, if not as cosmopolitan as he himself was.

Now the familiar limousine pulled up outside and the count swept in, wearing a dramatic cashmere hunting cape. My mother signaled to me to take it from him, and he poured it into my arms with its exquisitely soft kid lining. The count's eyes sought and found mine for a split second, and I quickly looked away from this *frisson* of interest, blushing furiously.

His appearance created a stir among Mama's seamstresses, hiding behind their hands and peeking at this celebrity in their midst. Philippa and the two children flooded up to greet and embrace him. He kissed the countess affectionately and dutifully, meanwhile subtly reaching back and squeezing Philippa's pert behind as she held up the children for their kiss. Philippa smiled at him sweetly. I didn't dare look at my mother who may have missed that quick motion, preoccupied as always with this or that garment she carried with her everywhere.

The count strode commandingly through the staring women and into my father's study. I heard the two men greet each other and plunge right into a discussion of the latest conflicts, speculating on the next moves of Hitler and the British. I yearned to join them in conversation, but the closest I could get was helping Mama prepare a decanter of brandy and our best crystal glasses on a tray, which she carried in herself.

Back in the front room, Philippa was chattering about Hedy Lamarr, the beautiful Austrian-born movie star, as the children played at her feet. This was what we women discussed while the men debated American capitalism versus Soviet collectivism and the theories of John Maynard Keynes, the British economist.

". . . and they say she had an affair with Robert Taylor and William Holden both. And with the whole football team of the Los Angeles University . . ." Philippa said, laughing with frank relish at the debauchery.

"Philippa!" My mother put a finger to her lips, indicating the children. But of course we knew her real concern was for my own impressionable ears.

"What does she need with all those men?" my mother said, "when she could be a happily married woman?" At this, Philippa and the countess exchanged an amused glance.

"Oh Miriam, you're so . . . precious." The countess laughed.

"Old-fashioned, you mean," said my mother. "I admit I am."

"Yes, but in such a wonderful way," Philippa said.

"I'm more worldly than you give me credit for," said my mother, trying for a knowing smile. At this Philippa and the countess shrieked with laughter.

The children suddenly fussed and spatted. Philippa expertly separated them and plunked the little girl onto her lap. I came forward to help distract them. "Anton," said Philippa, "be gentle with your sister." Philippa gazed keenly at me as she played with the child. "Mrs. Mielstone, Daniela is so beautiful! She reminds me of one of those deep crimson roses growing in your yard." All turned to look at me measuringly. The sudden attention brought the blood coursing up to my face.

"Me," continued Philippa, "I'm afraid I'm just one of those pale little tea roses. Hardly a blush and then fade away, la la . . ."

The countess listened wryly. "Hardly a blush is very apt, my dear." She and Philippa laughed while I looked around helplessly.

"Oh no! You're . . . just beautiful," I blurted to Philippa with utter sincerity, and she smiled at me through her laugher.

The little girl Katerina piped up, "What kind of rose am I, Pilipa?"

"Why, you're a miniature pink rosebud, my darling!" Philippa kissed the child with real affection.

"Am I a rose, too?" Anton blurted, jealous of his sister and the attention she was getting. We laughed.

"Not a rose, Anton," said Philippa, "but a powerful branch of oak!" How characteristic of Philippa to turn his envy and anxiety into an admirable trait.

"With his father's wooden head!" muttered the countess *sotto voce*, and again, she and Philippa screeched with laughter while my mother and I feigned interest in the floor.

"And speaking of wooden heads," said the countess to my mother, "Philippa's father—"

"Oh, Countess, spare them," said Philippa with a pleading grin.

". . . gambled and drank away a fortune, would you believe? And left his poor daughter to make her way as a governess."

"Yes, poor little me. Adrift in the cold, cruel world . . ." Philippa's eyes met those of the countess, who smiled cynically and indulgently. I could tell that she liked Philippa, another girl of slender means who had not had the countess' own luck and opportunistic daring.

"Since Philippa arrived, we have been a happier family than ever before," said the countess. "The children . . . and their father, too." She threw another significant glance at Philippa who was, to my surprise, blushing a little. "All thanks to our lovely damask rose here," the countess continued. "My husband gives me lots of money to buy these pretty dresses . . . and to travel far away to exotic places."

I gawked a little, puzzled at the mysterious subtext of this conversation among worldly women. How I craved to be in the know and understand their multiple layers of meaning.

"Daniela," said my mother finally, "will you please go fetch me a . . . bobbin? And more black thread."

"With the war approaching, we should stock up on all things black," the countess said. I turned to leave the room.

"I'll go with my crimson rose," said Philippa. "I need to stretch my legs." She turned to the children. "Now you both stay right there, and don't make trouble."

Philippa put her arm around me, and we walked out together—but not so quickly that I missed the thoughtful look on Mama's face.

Philippa and I stopped at the supply closet with its rows of thread and ribbon and boxes of buttons—a world in itself that I used to sit and stare into when I was a child, for my mother never allowed us to play with these thousands of little gems. The only time she had ever slapped my hand was when I had grabbed a handful of silver buttons defiantly after being told to leave them alone.

"Those are our living, Daniela. They are not toys. I told you before, and yet you disobey me." Mama had grabbed my plump little hand, desperately clutching my prize and pried it open. The buttons had fallen onto the floor and rolled away in all directions. Mama slapped my open palm gently, not even enough to sting. But I was so shocked at this unexpected discipline that I screamed and cried piteously, not for the pain but for the idea that I had so displeased and disappointed my mother.

I never open the closet door without thinking of that moment. I understood eventually that the contents of the closet represented a major investment for the family business—exquisite, hand-painted cameo buttons and others made from precious stones—all of this not for us but for the wealthy, destined to decorate that world of privilege and luxury that we could only serve and not inhabit.

Now, as I reached in for a spool of black satin thread and a new bobbin, Phillipa surveyed me curiously. "Perhaps someday you'll be a designer, too?"

I laughed and shook my head. "I have no talent for this. I learned that long ago." At Philippa's curious look,

I added, out of bruised pride, "I'm going to be a doctor."

"A doctor! That's unusual."

"But why should it be? I want to help conquer diseases. End suffering."

Philippa gave a little laugh. "Oh all that, of course. But what about marrying? Traveling? The war can't go on forever."

"I wonder if we ever will travel again. The world is exploding."

Philippa sighed. "So what are smart, beautiful, ambitious girls like us to do?"

"It seems that others will decide our fate," I said.

Philippa's face clouded and hardened. "If you let others decide your fate," she said intensely, "you'll never hold a scalpel."

She suddenly clutched my empty hand and closed the hand into a fist and shook the fist.

"Seize every chance to get what you want!" I looked at her questioningly; this version of Philippa seemed so different from the offhand, lighthearted nanny I knew. This wiser, bitterer Philippa intended me to take her seriously. Both of our smiles faded. I shrank back a little before Philippa's sudden, serious intensity.

"Seize the life you truly want," she said to me. "Like the countess did, and like I intend to as well, with every chance I get."

"I . . . I think I understand," I said. Philippa still clutched my hand, even hurting it a little. She nodded once, as if we had just made some sort of pact. Then she shook off her mood, opened my hand, and took it playfully.

"But come," she said, "Show me your beautiful garden!

I have never been behind your home."

"Of course," I said and conducted her outdoors. We descended the back stairs into our summery garden, rich with flowers and fruit trees. Philippa had by now returned to her frivolous, lighthearted mode.

"How splendid all this is. It makes me yearn for England."

I picked her a gardenia, and Philippa put it in her hair behind her ear. The scent was almost dizzying in the late afternoon heat.

"Thank you for the advice," I said. "And for making me feel pretty. I never do, you know."

Philippa beamed. "You'll soon be swimming in compliments," she said. "But do me a favor and don't get married to the first man who wants you."

I almost mentioned *Lady Chatterley's Lover* but stopped myself. I ducked my head shyly and shrugged. I had never even seen a man of course—only a picture of Michelangelo's "David." I had not known what to think.

I mustered my courage. "Tell me," I said, "what you know about men. Tell me everything."

Philippa laughed out loud. "I will tell you all you want to know," she whispered in my ear. "But I cannot do that here. We'll have to think of a way to meet somewhere outside your mother's vigilant gaze."

I began to giggle uncontrollably, and Philippa joined in, in the way that young women together have done since ancient days.

Knowing what I know now, I can picture her that night in the count's bedroom with its massive four-poster canopy bed, sumptuous satin sheets, and down pillows. I think of her cavorting with the count and slyly informing him, "I think I may have found us a little playmate, Antonin."

"Tell me," he would have said. "Do you mean that little Jewish ingenue with the arresting hazel-green eyes? Is she even sixteen yet?"

"Perhaps just. She's a perfect mix of innocence, curiosity, rebellion—and conspiracy."

And the count would have laughed with lustful delight as he played with Philippa's long, silken blonde hair, draped across her slinky body.

"Why don't you invite her to tea?"

"I may do. But it's not simple. Her mother is—"

"Yes, you needn't tell me. Such a morally proper woman."

"As all mothers ought to be."

"It only makes seduction more . . . piquant."

"Yes, well, it may take a little time to negotiate . . ."

"Ah . . ." The count grew serious and reached for a cigarette. "Time, you see, is what we do not have. The political situation is getting worse by the hour. I don't know how much longer I can hold off the Nazis. With them it's always now now now. They can't wait to get their greedy hands on everything Romanian. And they won't be satisfied until all Europe is awash in blood."

"Ah."

"So . . . if you have any plans for your little apprentice, you had better put them into play at once." Philippa covered his hand with hers.

"I'm making arrangements to leave," said the count, "until the war is past. Nothing awaits us here but death—and who knows if there'll even be anything to return to."

Philippa glanced around at the luxury, the lighted

candles reflected in the gilt-edged, beveled mirrors.

"Yes," said the count bitterly, "take a good look at the past. Yours and mine. Everyone's." Philippa flung her arms around the count, and they embraced with desperate passion.

An Apt Pupil

AND NOW, imagine a sunny late afternoon with a few billowing clouds high aloft, gentle and benign under the infinite sky. Seen from a distance a slender young man of nearly nineteen walked down the tree-lined road toward our home, holding a book. Dark hair, soft and wavy, brushed his collar. A downy mustache on his shapely upper lip betrayed his youth, but his gray-eyed gaze was steady and intelligent, hinting at determination and even willfulness. He reached the portico of our home, paused for a moment, took a breath, and knocked.

My father opened the door. Behind him were my mother and little Jacob, all gawking.

As my father smiled with affectionate recognition, Mihail spoke shyly.

"How do you do, Mr. . . . Mielstone. I-I'm the tutor that—"

"Of course, I recognize Mihail! How do you do! Ah, you've grown up!" My father reached out and pumped Mihail's hand.

Jacob elbowed forward. "Do you know math games?"

Mihail beamed down at him. "Do I know math games!"

"Hooray! Come and play. Right now!"

Jacob grabbed Mihail's hand before the young man was even inside the door. Quickly, Mihail touched the mezuzah on the door frame and allowed Jacob to pull him inside, where he almost bumped into my mother, coming forward with her own hand extended.

"Jacob! Show some manners!"

"But I am, Mama. I'm making him welcome!"

"He's not here to play games with *you*," my mother said. "Perhaps you can play the violin for him later." Jacob laughed again. Mihail grinned, and Mama smiled indulgently.

"Jacob's been lonely since the Romanians closed the *cheder*...."

"I know what they've done," said Mihail. "I hear everything. I've been fortunate enough to study in Paris this past couple of years, but I know what's been happening."

"So we heard," said Papa. "But what a time to return."

"I . . . missed my family," Mihail said. "I couldn't stay away any longer." My father patted his shoulder.

"Come in, come in, and sit down," said my mother. "Have cookies and tea."

They conducted Mihail into the parlor, where a table was set with every treat in the house. My father watched Mihail with a little smile as the young man discreetly glanced around, looking for me. But I was well hidden behind the kitchen door. My father gestured to Mihail.

"Here, let's sit and eat! If we wait for your student, we'll starve." He shouted at me as I disappeared up the staircase. "Daniela! Your education awaits!"

My mother entered and set down the steaming teapot. She looked at my father and shrugged. Mihail kept his eyes down.

Up in my bedroom I whipped off the childish dress I had put on and hurled it to the floor to join a large pile of rejected outfits. I had tried to style my hair, with poor results. My "sophisticated" upswept hairdo was lopsided and amateurish. It looked nothing like Philippa's.

"Dammit," I hissed, and pulled down the failed hair-do, sending pins and combs flying. I went to my bureau and dipped my hair into a cold basin. Down in the parlor, Mihail took a bite of a cookie and a sip of tea under the intent scrutiny of my whole family. Jacob was bursting to talk. I heard his chattering voice.

"Brothers and sisters I have none. This man's father is my father's son! Who is he? Quick, don't think too long!"

"What do you mean you have no sister?" My mother laughed. "God forbid!"

Mihail grinned. "That would be his own son."

Jacob beamed. "You are smart."

"Jacob, leave him alone," said my mother.

"I confess," said my father, "I was utterly baffled." He winked at Mihail.

As they ate, I finally descended the stairs. I had chosen a plain, fitted black skirt and simple white blouse. My wet hair was shaped to my head, and I had tied a red bow at the back. At least it tamed the waves.

Jacob spotted me first. "Oh, there she is! Daniela, come have tea with your tutor. He's good at games. And whatever happened to your hair?"

Slowly, Mihail raised his eyes to meet mine. Our gazes locked, and Einstein's entire cosmos stopped as we stared at one another. Mihail's eyes burned through me.

Do you believe in love at first sight? Some portray

love as a cyclone wrenching your soul from its moorings. But for me, love was a sunrise. From the fierce night of my isolation, a light now glowed, and soon the horizon was aflame. Even years later, I watch the sunrise each morning and think of Mihail.

Now I took my place at the table and looked helplessly at my cup of tea, frozen with shyness and afraid that my hand would shake if I picked it up. My father and Jacob, oblivious, were already working a math game from Mihail's book on a piece of paper. Somehow, I managed to make small talk and comport myself decently. But I could not bring myself to meet his gaze again.

As I rose to help my mother clear the table, my father and Mihail began to talk seriously.

"You'll stay for supper after Daniela's lesson, won't you, Mihail?" My mother asked. Listening, I froze.

"Of course he will," my father shouted into the kitchen.

My mother busied herself putting away dishes and didn't look at me.

"He seems very smart," Mama said. "I think he has a lot to teach you."

I closed my eyes blissfully; my entire head was spinning, and I was only vaguely aware of my hands lifting glasses and putting away food.

But now in the parlor, I heard Mihail speaking to my father in a much different voice than the polite guest of only moments ago.

"People here are talking nonsense," Mihail said. "They try to reassure themselves, 'as bad as things are, at least we're not at war yet.' But right now, right here in Yedinitz, the Gestapo is training the Iron Guard. And they're not training them to catch butterflies."

"What would you have us do?" said my father.

"At this point, it's too late to run. We must stand and prepare to fight."

"Fight?" My father indicated little Jacob, working on a math problem.

"He's not too young to pull a trigger," Mihail said. Jacob looked up and grinned at Mihail as my father recoiled in horror.

"I am not so sure as you are," said my father. "What do we have to gain by violence?"

"This is not about what we gain," said Mihail, "it is what we are about to lose. Do you have any doubt whatsoever about Hitler's intentions?"

"But you firebrands are talking pure suicide," said my father. "You don't know who you're dealing with."

"And I believe just the opposite," said Mihail. "It is the older people who do not know, or do not wish to know."

I entered, and Mihail's eyes rested on me. I avoided his gaze, trying not to breathe too quickly because I was dizzy already. My father rose.

"Come, you two. Mother set you up a table in the living room."

Papa conducted us into the living room, which was reserved only for guests. A round table had been set up with writing paper and a lamp, as the sun was beginning to set.

Slowly, as if in a trance, Mihail and I sat down across the table from each other. Jacob had followed us in, but my father shepherded him quickly out.

"Stop hovering, Jacob. Daniela has to concentrate. This is very important."

So finally we were alone. I sat stiffly. Mihail extended a pencil. "Perhaps we should begin."

I took the pencil as he opened a book and began instructing me in algebra. Fortunately I had been a good math student, and this work was easy for me—because I was only listening with half of my consciousness. The lamp glowed between us, and I watched Mihail, not the paper.

". . . so, we need to factor this trinomial by grouping," Mihail said. "First, we split the middle term into two terms. And see? There's your common factor between the first two and last two terms . . ." He looked up and caught my eye. "I think you understand this already, but the difficulty of these equations rises sharply when we get into . . ." he stopped, smiling. "So you really want to be a doctor."

"With all my heart!" I looked at him keenly now. "Why? Do you think I'm slow?"

He began to protest, and I seized my pencil. "I'll factor your trinomial for you!" I wrote furiously. "There! X equals the quantity two and a minus six."

Mihail burst out laughing. "You know this well already. Good! Now we can advance even faster."

"Don't worry that I'll be a waste of time for you."

"You could never be a waste of time." He put his hand over mine. At that moment, if he had told me to trade my career for the burning gates of hell, I would have leaped forward joyously. But to my shock, he leaned toward me, and his lips brushed mine very softly. This in my own parents' home, within a few feet of my father, conveniently dozing in his armchair!

I nearly jumped out of my seat but managed not to

make a sound. Riveted with shock, I sat staring at the trinomial. Somehow I knew that the equation of my own life had just changed.

My lips stung and throbbed from that stolen caress as if bathed in horseradish. I must be a devil woman, I thought, to provoke such brazen conduct in a studious young man. I realized that I stood at the precipice, but even so, I had some sense of propriety, or rather, strategy. Not to give myself too easily—I knew that at least from all my reading. I determined to suppress my desire for the greater reward that awaited: that of spending my life with Mihail.

Quickly, I turned to look around. In his study, my father was still somnolent in his armchair. I could just hear my mother in the kitchen with Jacob. Our secret was safe.

Somehow, we finished our lesson. Everything seemed so normal, and yet everything had changed forever. Had that kiss actually happened? Or had I just imagined it? Had I become psychotic, believing what was not?

I heard my mother call out: "Students! Come have dinner. Everything is ready." Mihail and I rose from the study table and closed the books. To my surprise, my legs still worked properly.

"Daniela," said my father, "go and help your mother serve."

I fled to the kitchen, glad to be safely alone to think about my new secret.

"Well," I heard my father say to Mihail, "how did our Daniela do? Is there hope?"

"She shows a real aptitude," Mihail said with great seriousness.

I bit my lips, wanting to laugh, or scream, or cry out—I

didn't know which.

Mama and I carried dishes to the table, and I carefully avoided Mihail's eyes as I balanced the food. At last I sat next to him, where my mother indicated. I could only look down at my plate and wonder how I would ever bring myself to eat.

"So the Jews of Europe are kaput, are we?" my father said.

My mother set down a plate of food and turned on Papa. "Schmuel, let us have a peaceful meal, at least. How can you speak this way in front of these young people with their whole lives ahead of them? Please no more talk of war and madness."

"We could go to London with the countess," Jacob said to Mihail. "She wants to take us with her. We could go right now."

"That would be wise," said Mihail.

"But how can we just leave everything behind?" said Mama. "Our home? My business? My clients? Our friends we've known all our lives? Our families?"

I could tell that Mihail was seething. I met his eyes and with my gaze encouraged him to speak out. Already, I believed in him. I would follow him anywhere.

"I don't mean to be disrespectful," Mihail said, "but Jacob and Daniela are all the more reason to leave now if you can."

"Oh," said Mama, "so you're one of them, too."

"I believe the Jews must fight. Yes."

For an endless moment we all sat in silence. I hoped that my parents would not now forbid him from the house, now that they knew he was a "firebrand."

"Perhaps Hitler will be assassinated," said my mother.

"We should be so lucky," said Papa.

Mihail could keep silent no longer. "By not preparing for the worst, we ensure it. We've already waited too long to arm ourselves."

"What am I hearing? Arm ourselves?" said Mama.

"But with what?" said my father.

Mihail brandished a steak knife as Jacob's eyes widened with delight and our parents recoiled. "Guns, knives, bombs—whatever we can steal or build," Mihail said. "Or buy. We are in a fight to the death."

"I can't listen to this," said my mother.

"But Mama," I said, "we must listen! We can't hide from the truth."

Under the table, Mihail suddenly placed his hand gently upon my knee. I gasped and swayed in my chair.

"Enough!" shouted Mama. "This violent talk is making Daniela ill. She's very high-strung, Mihail. You are as welcome here as our own son, but please, try not to upset this girl. She still has to study tonight when you leave."

Mihail nodded and smiled, once again, a perfectly proper young tutor. I felt faint. His hand was still on my knee. "I apologize," said Mihail to my mother as his hand explored upward toward my thigh, "if I have upset anyone. I am grateful for your hospitality. I'll be leaving now." At that moment, I couldn't have cared less whether all of Europe disappeared without a trace. I thought to myself, what would Lady Chatterley do? And then, in my own parents' living room, I placed my hand over his.

"These are the hardest of times," Mama said. "And yet we still have to live and work, not give up on the future. We Jews will get by somehow. We always have. We always do."

Mihail's smile faded at my mother's words, but he rose and continued thanking my parents as he gathered his books and papers.

"Daniela, where are your manners?" said Mama. "Show your guest to the door. And thank him for the lesson."

I wobbled to my feet. "Of course, Mama." I conducted Mihail to the front room, feeling his eyes on me, warming my back like sunbeams. We walked outside onto the front porch. The air was still balmy under a waxing moon.

The moment the door closed behind us, Mihail put his arms around my waist and kissed me again and again. The insects thrummed in the garden; the stars glowed bright as candles in the rapidly cooling air as love and desire blazed up inside me like a torch. A mulchy aroma issued from the ground, and I shivered, all reserve collapsing. My fiery will came under his sway, and I was consumed.

I went to bed immediately with a fever and a spinning head, all thoughts of equations and botanical taxonomy gone. I could not even read a novel; the letters blurred and danced impishly and chaotically. A buzzing whine sounded in my ears. I had heard of rivers suddenly flowing in the opposite direction after some geological cataclysm, an earthquake or an avalanche. I was such a river, wrenched from my course, rushing toward a fate over which I had not the slightest control.

Before that night, I had no time for fashion. But now, I could think of nothing but how to make myself alluring. Already, I was planning where and how to give myself to him.

Now Mama would stand behind me, twisting my

turbulent hair into a snood like a fashionable New York lady. She even left a wealthy matron standing in her corset to help me dress, arranging a little scarf at my neck.

My poor mother nearly sparkled with delight at the change in me. If she only knew. I looked up at her, and we looked into the mirror together. Mama's face shined with innocent conspiratorial delight and love; her Daniela was blossoming. I wish I could say I felt guilty for my carnality and deception, but guilt was far from my mind.

I sat now with Mihail studying and watched him as he looked down at a book. He glanced up and caught my eye.

"You're blushing," he said to me.

"And you make it worse!"

He laughed, then sobered. A sad, bitter look came into his eyes.

"It's all so . . . irrelevant."

"My education?"

He shook his head sadly. "No . . . it's just that we're leading such normal lives in the teeth of destruction. To be sitting here, counting . . . memorizing, munching cookies while . . ."

"You would rather have all the Jews building bombs?"

"Of course I would."

"Mihail," I said, "there's such violence in you."

"It's our enemies who are violent. They're monsters; their evil knows no bounds."

I looked at him sadly, and he put his hand over mine. I drew a deep breath, as if to banish all gloomy thoughts. "Well, we aren't going to solve the world's problems this afternoon. Tell me about your family."

He smiled, too, trying to find and recapture our joy.

"I have one brother who attends art school in New York. And my older brother studies physics at home."

"And what do you want to do? Certainly not be a tutor forever."

Mihail hesitated. "Somehow, I can't . . . think past the war. Anyway," he sighed, "my father's a Communist like yours, but even more so. He still carries the card, even after Stalin sold out to Hitler."

"How can he?"

"Because he's a true believer. In spite of Stalin's lies and murder, my father thinks Communism is the only hope for a just society."

"Communism is fatally flawed," I ventured, my heart pounding at the risk.

"Oh?" Mihail frowned. "What has the human race had in its place? Monarchy? Religious tyranny?"

"What about democracy?"

Mihail scoffed. "For sale to the highest bidder. The tyranny of the rich and corrupt, just cloaked in fine words."

"And tyranny doesn't exist under Communism?"

"It's not the fault of Communism itself. It's the human element."

"But all systems are run by people!" I said, feeling dismayed at myself. Why did I keep defying him? What if he turned away from me? "Usually the wrong people!" I added, to soften my answer.

To my relief, he laughed. "Yes, the wrong people. At last we have found common ground."

I could have hugged him. "Oh, why do people have to worship anything at all?"

Mihail grinned. "When you say that, I know that you

are the true love that—"

"That? . . ."

"That God has sent me."

We burst out laughing, tried to stifle it, and kissed recklessly.

"We'll get caught," I murmured. But he continued kissing me.

Days later, I looked out the window and to my delight saw the Countess Kányádi and Philippa with the two children, all arriving in the countess' cream-colored Daimler.

"It's the countess! And Philippa!" I shouted.

"Yes. She's here for another fitting." My mother paused, intrigued. "Why so excited? The countess has put on weight is all, so we have many alterations. She worries about the war and eats to calm herself, she says. But when she gains, we gain!" Mama laughed at her little word play, but I only nodded, not really listening. I raced to open the door, curtsy to the countess, then seized Philippa's hand.

"Philippa!"

"Daniela! I hardly recognized you." She glanced analytically at my newly fashionable outfit. I didn't care anymore what people said about me. I only dressed to please Mihail.

"She's grown up overnight," Philippa told my mother. "And I love your hair," she said to me.

"Look at me," said the countess, "a fat pig!"

"What are you talking about? I see nothing!" said Mama. "You're far too hard on yourself."

I spoke *sotto voce* to Philippa. "Come, I have to talk to you." I began to lead her out of the room. Philippa turned to the children.

"Sit here, and don't move," she said to them. "Or I may

get sent back to England!"

"No! No!" the children chorused. They sat and grabbed some yarn to play cat's cradle.

"Daniela! Go make tea," said Mama.

"I'll help her," Philippa said quickly as we two hurried to the kitchen.

"Jacob!" called my mother. "Jacob, where are you? Come play your violin for the countess. She finds your music relaxing." In the hallway, we ran into Jacob, seething.

"Relaxing?! My music is *relaxing*? Is that what she thinks?" He was startled at the sight of Philippa. "Oh!" he cried, "pardon me. I am sorry."

Philippa laughed and put her arms around him. "Your playing is not a bit *relaxing*, Jacob. It's thrilling and moving."

Jacob's face lit up like a candle. I could see that he had a crush on her, and my heart overflowed with love for them both. "I'll play for you, Philippa. I'll play anything you like."

I smiled gratefully at Philippa as Jacob ran for his violin. He brought his music stand into the sewing room and instantly dove into a turbulent virtuoso piece. The countess and Mama jumped a little at the pyrotechnics, and the seamstresses giggled.

Grateful for the distraction, Philippa and I ran into the kitchen to get the tea things. The moment we were alone, I grabbed her hand.

"I have to tell you something. I'm in love!" The words tumbled out with no restraint.

Philippa laughed. "I knew it! The moment I saw you." Her eyes lit up with that joy of intrigue universal to women of all ages, eras, and cultures. I realized suddenly how isolated she must have felt here in this Bessarabian hamlet, remote from her own friends and society. I later learned that her family, minor nobles, had fallen into poverty as a result of her father's chicanery and gambling.

"I have . . . become . . . very . . . interested in my tutor," I faltered.

"How irresistible," she said. "Tell me everything."

"I've never felt this way. I've turned into a . . . I don't know. A . . . libertine. Maybe I'm crazy."

Philippa smiled knowingly. She took my hand, her eyes dancing with mischief and excitement. "Tell me all."

I turned away and pretended to fuss with the tea things; my hands were trembling. "I can't tell anyone else how I feel. They would never understand. Oh Philippa, I'm so glad I know you."

"I feel the same," she said. "I've been so lonely here. I hardly know anybody besides the count and countess. There's really nobody to tell my secret thoughts to. And now I have you."

Impulsively and a little awkwardly, I embraced her. I was not accustomed to such intimacy with one that I hardly knew. I caught a vague, exquisite scent, a flower I didn't recognize. Beneath her silky blouse, her slender body was light, almost insubstantial, as if she were some spirit, a fairy. My life was suddenly so changed—who was I now and where? I felt as if I were walking about in a dream.

"Philippa, he's the most brilliant, the handsomest . . . I . . . was unable to study. He must have found me stupid."

"Not likely. Who is he?" She smiled knowingly. "Have you . . ."

I searched her eyes, flushing furiously under her keen gaze. "Only kissed," I blurted. "But I . . . I want to be his. Every part of me cries out for him. I don't care about anything but him."

Philippa's smile became a humorous pout. "I'm jealous! You have someone to love so passionately! But truly, I'm happy for you. Who is this amazing man to have possessed you so thoroughly? Does he live here in town?"

"His name is Mihail," I whispered. "Mihail Borowiak. He is the tutor that my parents hired for me."

Philippa suddenly froze. Her mouth dropped open a bit before she caught herself and reassumed her excited, conspiratorial air. But something had changed; she seemed surprised, even shocked. She stared harder at me, deeply and searchingly, tilting her head to the side. "Philippa," I almost cried out, "you know him. Please! Tell me everything. What have you heard?"

"I've heard that he has the best cock in Yedinitz," Philippa said coolly. I must have screamed, because my mother came running in with a bolt of fabric trailing onto the floor. Philippa composed herself. "Daniela is all right, Mrs. Mielstone," she said. "I told her a joke, that's all." My mother returned to the sewing room, shooting me a look.

Philippa smiled at me again, trying to recapture our conspiratorial glee. "You've chosen well. Don't worry." Now she embraced me but briskly and hard. Her breath came fast, as if she were holding something inside at a great effort.

Despite my inexperienced confusion, I easily sensed that my news had caught her unprepared, and she was unable to control her feelings completely.

Just at that moment, Mama called in, "Daniela! Make

some watercress sandwiches and bring up the new apricot jam. Her Highness is a little hungry." I heard the countess laughing.

Philippa rolled her eyes. "*Always* hungry," she whispered and gave a quick, tight smile.

But I could not let go of my question. "I have to know everything. How do you know him, Philippa, tell me. *Tell* me!" I felt like shaking her.

By now Philippa had regained her self-possession. "Whatever do you want to know?" she said lightly. I searched her face with dawning realization, and she returned my gaze boldly. So! I thought. Does she love him, too?

"I mean," Philippa said, "there is nothing . . . of that nature between us anymore, of course. I wouldn't deny knowing him."

"There is something between you and him," I said. "Are you lovers?"

Philippa laughed. "I won't lie. We saw one another socially after we had met . . . in a . . . in a shop. I was buying food. Anyway, it was long ago."

"You weren't here long ago," I couldn't help reminding her.

"Whatever the time was . . . obviously a relationship was impossible. He is the son of dedicated Communists, you know."

"I do," I said. "His family is more radical even than my father."

"He despises everything the count and countess stand for. Why . . . if it were up to him their lands would be seized and collectivized, given to the peasants . . ."

I grinned at this. "I know his politics, Philippa. He

isn't quite as great an ogre as that."

"That's what you think. You don't really know him, Daniela. Don't make the mistake of believing what your heart tells you. He is . . . quite unprincipled."

"Unprincipled?" I couldn't apply that word to the Mihail I knew. But suddenly I thought of his hand on my knee at my parents' very table. And . . . other liberties he had taken—not without my own eager complicity.

I closed my eyes under waves of confusion.

"His family is far from 'penniless, principled idealists,' you know, living only for the Communist utopia—the rule of the proletariat and all that rhetoric he has probably thrown at you by now." She sounded unaccountably bitter.

My mother called again from the other room as Philippa and I stared at one another. "Daniela! What are you doing in there? Telling tales? Where is our tea?" I immediately turned back to the tea things, my hands trembling as I fumbled with the leaves and the food.

Philippa saved me, shouting out, "It's all my fault, Mrs. Mielstone. I'm hopelessly clumsy today. Why I just nearly burned myself."

Philippa and I arranged the tea things quickly, neither of us too steady. It was one thing to confide intimate secrets to someone, I was learning, and quite another how they responded to it.

"You are," Philippa said, composed now, ". . . in the hands of a very capable tutor. He will educate you thoroughly." I didn't miss the irony, but I didn't care.

"I . . . I love him," I said.

Philippa suddenly grasped my childish, chapped hands with her own slender, elegant hands. "Then do so," she said. "Love him with all your heart."

For a moment, she and I almost glared at one another. Then I took her hands in mine.

"I don't care about the past, Philippa. I am not worldly, but I have read . . . all about love, and I accept its risks and dangers."

Philippa threw her arms around me. "How I adore you, Daniela. You are a spirited, courageous young woman—in a time that cries out for people like you. You are not a timid conformist like . . . so many these days."

I felt a surge of pride in myself. Instead of scolding and cautioning me, it was as if Philippa was praising my contrariness and independent spirit—the traits I had battled all my life. "Thank you, Philippa," I said, meaning it with all my heart.

"You have the makings of a . . . heroine," Philippa said. "Like a Tolstoy heroine." The only Tolstoy heroine that came to my mind was, of course, Anna Karenina, and I had to laugh. She was not exactly the appropriate type of heroine to recommend to a fifteen-year-old girl. But suddenly I felt reckless, craving my freedom from the suffocating niceties and proprieties I had grown up with. We both laughed. I took a deep breath.

"But Philippa," I said, my hands rapidly making sandwiches, "I'm like a prisoner here. We only see each other when my parents are nearby. We grab some time before he departs. It's like being in a cage for both of us."

Philippa laughed now with delight. "I can arrange to give you both all the privacy you will ever need."

I looked at her with fierce gratitude, and an agreement was wordlessly forged there, over the tea and watercress sandwiches.

Sweet Deception

SEVERAL DAYS LATER, up in my room, I dressed myself carefully and chose a light coat. Mama entered, holding the article she was sewing, as usual. I had readied
myself for the most important day of my life, so far.

"Where are you going this morning?" Mama said.

"Just . . . on a bicycle ride, Mama. I need some fresh
air."

"You look very nice for a bicycle ride," said Mama.
"It's the best thing for you. You spend way too much time
cooped up in your room reading books."

My mother lovingly buttoned my coat and kissed me
on both cheeks. I avoided her eyes, but suddenly felt the
need to hug her. Then I dashed out, my eyes suddenly
filled with tears. At least, I told myself, you still have a
conscience.

Out on the main street of Yedinitz, people were walking back and forth, doing their errands, looking worried,
and doubtlessly talking about the war that grew closer
every day. But I didn't pay attention to them. A few people waved at me, friends of my parents who believed they
were greeting a virtuous, obedient Jewish daughter. But
they were not; and it gave me pleasure to think that.

Just outside of town, the land changed as I approached the count's estate. I had been here several times with my mother over the years when the countess was entertaining and had been unable to come to our home for last-minute touch-ups before a party or dinner. She depended on my mother to maintain her reputation as the best-dressed woman in the region, even though many of the other women were also wearing my mother's creations. Sometimes the countess would bring back fashions from Paris and London, and my mother would inspect these with a jaundiced eye looking for flaws in the workmanship.

The truth was, my mother's skills were easily comparable to the salons of Paris, but at a much-reduced price. The countess enjoyed having people comment on her "Paris" fashions that had been made right here in Yedinitz.

The count's castle was said to date back to the eighth century, but today it looked more like a modern luxury hunting lodge, which was the purpose it served for the count. There were offices but the main living quarters were actually modeled after Hitler's Berghof retreat in the town of Berchtesgaden amid the Obersalzberg mountains of Austria.

Panoramic windows in the main room looked out on our own forests and hills rather than the imposing Alps, but like the Berghof, the estate had a large terrace used for entertaining in the summer, bedecked with those colorful, resort-style canvas umbrellas that Hitler favored.

The entrance hall even had the same cactus plants in majolica pots as decorated Hitler's Berghof. Also similar was the light jade-green color scheme and rooms full of antique furniture. The main dining room was paneled in costly wood—my mother said every time she walked into the place, she felt the malevolent insanity of Hitler reflected there.

The count maintained a large library furnished with what my mother called ponderous Teutonic furniture, a massive globe, and a vast red marble fireplace mantel. He even maintained, as did Hitler, a screening room for entertaining guests with Hollywood movies and home movies, too, of the count and countess on their travels. These were known for being excruciatingly boring, as most home movies are to those who are not starring in them. With all the picture windows, though, the place was impressive, and the count spent a lot of money keeping it maintained even when the family was away. The countess and Philippa were the same sort of highly sociable person, and so they tried to keep parties and events going all the time. When those were not enough, they would even think up and stage plays and entertainments.

But this morning I was going to a different part of the estate. As I navigated the dirt roads, I heard horses and knew I was on the right path. I dismounted my bike and walked it down the path, not knowing how I would explain my presence there to the servants. But Philippa had, as good as her word, arranged that I would not encounter any of the staff.

Just a few dozen yards from the stables, I finally reached the groom's quarters. The count had once been very "horsey," but because of the war, he had stopped breeding them, and horse shows were out of the question now. So because the count had scaled down his equestrian activities, several grooms' quarters had been standing empty all year. The horses were exercised, but otherwise the area stood deserted, awaiting the return of peace.

When I reached the main quarters, Philippa sprang out and greeted me with conspiratorial delight. I laid my bike aside and went with her into a small structure that stood apart from the main buildings.

I saw at once that Philippa had been as good as her word. The room was neat, with a closet, hooks for tackle, and a small desk. The large bed was freshly made. Beside it was a small stand with a bottle of wine, two glasses, fruit, and cheese and crackers.

Mihail was standing at the window and turned at our entrance, looking past Philippa at me. I felt my knees turn to rubber, but Philippa and Mihail welcomed me as if they were themselves the couple. Philippa whispered to me that the little house was a perfect trysting place, and I had no doubt that she and Mihail had spent many hours here. I could tell by the familiar way that he moved around that he knew the place well.

When my eyes encountered the bed, I looked away as if the sight of it burned them. I tried to master my embarrassment. This was indeed a tryst, and I might as well be honest with myself about it. All my reading of *Lady Chatterley's Lover* when I had wished to be Constance Chatterley herself was about to come true.

I thought, *Be careful what you wish for.* But I also felt filled with the power of rebellion. I was going to take my own life in my hands and do what my spirit and body wanted me to do. Who knew what the future held? I might not live out the year; from what I heard there was a very good chance that I would die. But for now I wanted to claim the sexual experiences and love that I believed I deserved.

"You won't be disturbed," Philippa said to me. "Don't worry about a thing." She embraced me and then gave Mihail a final parting look and was gone.

Alone together at last, as we had so many times wished for, Mihail and I were silent. I had imagined us rushing into one another's arms, but we were strangely reticent, standing apart, feeling more than a little awkward.

At last Mihail moved toward me, took my hand, and kissed it. We approached the bed slowly like a bride and bridegroom and stood before it.

"Well . . . so here I am, it seems. Here . . . *we* are," I said. Mihail didn't respond but looked closely at me. "Perhaps . . . I don't know . . . is this a . . . mistake?" I stammered.

"If you believe it is, you can leave," Mihail said. "Although I hope you don't. Only stay with me if you want to." Slowly, I raised my eyes to his, and he put his arms around me.

"My Daniela," he said. We kissed now without inhibition and slowly pulled the clothes from each other, exploring our bodies almost worshipfully. Knowing that war was imminent, this could be my only chance to truly live what I had spent so many hours fantasizing.

Mischievously, Philippa had left a bottle of wine for us. I was now sixteen, but my parents were very strict about my drinking only ceremonially or on holidays. So I had a sip, but I didn't want my senses to be dulled or to get drunk and risk behaving in a way that would annoy or even disgust Mihail.

And so our day began to pass in a slow, sensual flow of discovery and pleasure. With nobody to watch out for, I felt no shame or embarrassment, only wonder at the ability of my body to arouse and delight Mihail. My desire for him was so powerful that I knew what I was doing was right and good, even sacred. Yes, we were indulging in what nature had provided to give and take pleasure from another. I would pay a high price if we ever were discovered, so I wanted to gain the fullness of this lovemaking.

Even as a small child, I hadn't believed in the concept of religious sin. My books taught me that sensual love was a tribute to the work of God. And although I had absorbed my father's atheistic teaching, I understood that we were created to love one another, men and women, or even men together and women with women. But most of all now love was about Mihail and me.

As the day wore into afternoon, I fell totally under the spell of this young man. His skilled caresses aroused sexual responses in me that I could not have believed I was capable of, despite all of my reading. But now I understood Lady Chatterley and Anna Karenina and Madame Bovary and Colette—every character who dared to explore her own sexuality, to follow where the sensations led despite the taboos and rules of propriety and religion. I was the same type of woman.

Wherever he touched me, Mihail's hands and fingers seemed to leave a trail of flames in their wake; yes, I blazed under his caresses and discovered how easily he could bring me to orgasm—another sensation I had never known my body could deliver. And I shared the same pleasure in arousing him with my lips and my breasts and my vagina; shuddering and whispering, we tasted each other and pleasured each other without hesitation.

Looking back on that afternoon of exploration and immersion, I realized that I did indeed have a gift, as Mihail had said, smiling at my heedless, greedy pleasure.

"I'm amazed that you were able to keep your virginity for so long," he said. "You're untainted by all the artifacts of Victorian prudishness that our society has burdened us with."

"You think I'm a wanton?" I asked teasingly.

"Only in the best, most beautiful way," he said.

"It's your body, your hands and lips that lead me there. I wouldn't resist you even if I could. But I've never wanted another man, not like this. I can't imagine doing these things with anyone else."

"No," Mihail said, "but your power and desire will only grow as you get older. You're very beautiful, Daniela, and men are going to want you, especially in this lawless, chaotic time that's coming. Be careful, if I'm not around to protect you. I'll teach you how to protect yourself."

"With . . . guns?" I asked playfully, "and knives?"

"Yes. And with whatever your hands can grab." He looked at me intensely. "I've trained in France with other Jews, and I'll pass on the training to you. If we have the time. Daniela, this is not a frivolous thing. The war is very close. We may have only days before we're caught up in it. You will have to fight for your life, and for the lives of others, too. With whatever weapons you can find or make. And with your brain.

"In the days that are coming, you will have to be ready to kill if you want to live. I don't care about 'virtue' in a woman. It's a construct and completely artificial. But rape can damage and scar you emotionally. Yet whatever happens to you, you must be determined and ready to survive, and to help others survive."

"I understand," I said, a little frightened of him now, his intensity was so fierce.

"You know how I feel—that Jews must become warriors, Daniela. They want to kill us all, every one of us. Your parents are so ... naïve. They live in a dream world, and it is all about to shatter. What is happening right now in Poland is slaughter on a scale the world has never seen. Don't turn away, face it. Know it. Daniela, I want us to live through this, but if we can't I want us to take as many Nazis, as many of our enemies down with us as we can before we die."

By now I was crying, but Mihail would not comfort me yet. He wanted to infuse his determination and fierceness into me. I didn't realize it at the time, but that is exactly what he did. He gave me a sip of wine and then laughed suddenly, shedding his terrible anger as easily as taking off a coat.

"And now it's time to return to our pleasures. We have only begun."

I laughed, too, although my eyes were still red from the tears. But I felt braver and stronger. I would never let public opinion influence me again. I would never run from trivial whispers or gossip about my reputation.

"How I love being free," I said to him later. "I never want to be with any other man this way but you. You lit the tinder," I said, "when you put your hand on my knee."

We laughed. "I knew I was taking a terrible, reckless chance. But I wanted to ignite a fire in you. I wanted us to be one."

"And now we are. And God help us."

"Don't mention God," Mihail said. "There is either none, or he has abandoned us. And the war has only begun."

I realize now that I was precociously sexual; I was

curious, even licentious. I loved the sense of power I felt by arousing him and giving myself to him. *Who was this person I had become?* I wondered. Was this really me, Daniela, saying all of those frank, sexual words that Mihail seemed to take delight in teaching me? Wanting him inside me? He was a sensualist, too.

Mihail told me that he had carried on an affair with a woman in her thirties when he was only fourteen; this unhappily married woman had taught him exotic ways to arouse and satisfy her.

This piqued my curiosity—and a little jealousy, too. Who had she been and what had she meant to him? He laughed at my eagerness.

"You're very young, emotionally," he said. "Stay that way. I'll try not to embitter you. When love turns bitter, terrible things can happen."

We lay in bed, talking about everything that occurred to us. Mihail felt that fashion was a frivolous indulgence, I learned. He thought that our benefactors and protectors, the count and countess, were throwbacks to a medieval era. And that fashion in clothing, taken to this extreme, was a waste of resources, a pose, a pretense. He laughed at the countess and told me that everybody knew Philippa was the count's mistress.

"And yours, too," I said slyly.

"Did she tell you that?"

"All but."

"It's true. We were lovers. She is a very unhappy woman."

"But happier when she is with you," I said, stretching luxuriously. I felt very powerful right that minute.

"Don't let's talk about her. We have her generosity to

thank. And we need her discretion."

"Do you love her? Or did you?"

"Yes." This was not what I had expected.

Jealousy blazed up in me. "And perhaps you still do. Am I just an indulgence then, and is she your true love?"

"You are my true love. But people can love more than one."

"I forbid you to love her."

Mihail laughed. "You have nothing to worry about," he said.

"And as to fashion, people have always adorned themselves. Even primitive people, children, they make a canvas of their body, their skin, their hair."

Mihail smiled and nodded. "You're convincing me."

I grew shy. "Don't patronize me. Anyway I'm just chattering nonsense."

"You're not. You think. You understand things."

I blushed, "I don't know who I am anymore. Everything has changed." Suddenly, my eyes filled with tears. "Mihail . . . I'm lost!"

"Don't be. I have found you." He pulled me close and embraced me, kissing me tenderly. "Daniela, I love you more than life itself. Never be afraid."

Later, we drank the wine and nibbled fruit. Despite my caution, I grew tipsy. "No more! How will I explain to my mother?"

"Don't let her see you come in. You will have to learn to lie to her."

"I don't like to be deceitful."

Mihail laughed. "Then by all means, tell her you spent the day rolling about in bed with your tutor!"

I laughed, too. "You have to admit, Mihail, the

aristocracy comes in handy sometimes. What would we do without this groom's quarters?"

Mihail looked around, but now with contempt. "Nobles. They do nothing but waste limited resources. They take up land that should belong to the people for food and housing."

"People! You mean the peasants? All they want is for the Jews to suffer."

"Because they blame us for their poverty. That's how the aristocracy manipulates them." Mihail shook his head, full of contempt.

"The count lets his estate lie fallow so the quail and deer can multiply for his hunting parties. Meanwhile, poor children don't get enough protein, so they are sickly and stupid. If their parents are caught poaching, they rot in jail. Or pay fines from their wretched wages. They used to be hung." He lit a cigarette.

"Give me," I said, and he let me take a puff. Naturally I coughed. It was a foul, unpleasant feeling. Yet I took another puff.

"But how would my family live without the income we get from the countess and her rich friends?"

"Ah, the little bourgeoise," Mihail said.

I bridled. "Don't call me that!"

"We Jews beg for the crumbs they toss us. We lick their boots in the hope that they'll kick somebody else's ass. Oh, and we pray." He rolled his eyes. "For all the good that's ever done us. 'Please God, send us a *benevolent* tyrant. One who will only oppress and not murder us.'"

"Mihail, stop!"

"I just hope there are enough of us left to start over after this war."

I burst into tears, propelled by the wine. "Oh, you're so dark and bitter! Who are you? What have I done? If this is your love, take it back!"

"I cannot." Mihail took me in his arms and held me. "Love has no habitation but the heart. On the dark flood we catch awhile, cling, and are borne into the night..."

I lay in his arms and kissed him.

But later, as we were leaving, suddenly I turned—still tipsy—and confronted Mihail.

"How... did you and Philippa become friends?"

He laughed. "This again. I can see I will have to get used to it."

"Tell me!"

"Philippa belongs in the court of Charles II or Louis the XIV. She has everything a classic courtesan needs: wit, education, fearlessness..."

"I see," I said coldly.

"There's no reason to be jealous." Mihail took my face in his hands. "It's you I love. Anyway, it's too late. We belong to each other forever. Nothing that went before means anything. Now stop crying. Your family will suspect, and we'll lose our afternoons."

I smiled through my tears. And after all, I had Philippa to thank for the advice she gave me on avoiding pregnancy. She even bought me a diaphragm and taught me how to use it.

Now began a time that I look back on as the best in my life, those precious stolen hours in the groom's quarters. I became a common sight on the streets of Yedinitz on my bicycle. Perhaps people talked; perhaps everybody suspected; I don't know. As the weeks passed, that room became my second home. I no longer recognized myself.

When I think of our delightful lovemaking in the very eye of destruction, the earth around me trembles, even now, even here.

All around me, I could see the town preparing for *shabbat*, the sabbath. Women ran about selling and buying delicacies. But it meant nothing to us. My mother did her best to observe the holidays, but my father was a problem for her. He used the occasion to rail and rant against religion and against the "God" that he insisted was not only nonexistent according to the latest science of Einstein, but leading Jews astray into false beliefs.

I noticed the world as if from the corners of my eyes; nothing mattered to me but my love affair with Mihail and my studies. Because I was actually learning a lot more than sex from him. He was a brilliant student and knew amazing scientific theorems and mathematical proofs. He led me through the lessons in mathematics and physics just as he did in our lovemaking. I was an enthusiastic pupil.

When Mihail was instructing me, my poor little brother Jacob tried to join in the lessons, but he was too young to understand the increasingly complex theorems and proofs. He had been dismissed from his school for being Jewish, and his violin teacher was forbidden to teach a Jew, so his life had become limited and constricted, hanging around Mama's sewing room and playing increasingly mournful tunes on his violin, as if he felt the tragedy approaching. I wish now that I had paid more attention to him, but I was a woman obsessed.

It was *shabbat*, and my mother's warm, convivial table was surrounded by company, including Mihail of course. I gave him secret smiles that everybody probably saw as I helped my mother carry the dishes back and forth.

I know Mama saw the love blossoming between me and Mihail, and in her innocence she smiled knowingly at my father. For his past, Papa watched me and Mihail with a faintly quizzical look.

"So Mihail," Papa said unexpectedly at *shabbat* dinner, "how would you grade our little student?"

Mihail smiled and said, without a hint of irony, "She learns very quickly."

"So she'll make a good doctor?"

"A doctor!" said a dinner guest. "Is that what you want to be?"

"More than anything I want to be a doctor," I said.

Our guests nodded approvingly among themselves, but I saw many sad faces.

"How can people make plans for the future with war around the corner?" my parents' friend Mendel asked the table at large. "Now that Romania's forged this unholy alliance with the Nazis, they're very thirsty for Jewish blood."

Mama looked at Mendel and shook her head chidingly. "Mendel, not here, not now. At this table just for tonight, let there be peace and plenty." She looked around as the guests nodded and agreed.

"Yes," said Mendel, "let's take our pleasure without limits."

At that, my eyes met Mihail's for a brief, intense moment. That was exactly how we felt.

"God will not allow this destruction," said my poor mama.

But by now, Papa was drunk, and he was ready to speak out. "Woman," he said to Mama, "there is nothing that 'God' will not allow. Get it through your head." Papa drained his glass and lifted it at Mama to bring him more wine. "Come on, Jews!" he shouted. "Your glasses and plates are too full!" He took the decanter from Mama's hand and sloshed more wine into his glass; some of it splashed on the spotless tablecloth, but Papa didn't care or notice. Everybody hurriedly began to eat and drink.

Later, Mihail lingered as I helped clear the table. In the living room, we could hear the noise of discussions, arguments, and laughter.

I brought Mihail a glass of wine as he sat at the table watching me. He had lit a cigarette, a sign of his increasing comfort and belonging in the family. For a moment we were alone in the dining room, and I dared to put my arms around his shoulders as he sat and kiss the top of his head.

Mellowed by the wine, he turned and kissed me back. We were becoming inexcusably careless, because seconds later, Mama walked in and nearly caught us kissing. That would have caused her intense consternation and embarrassment in a house full of guests.

But suddenly, for the first time in my life, I yearned for tradition. I wanted to be Mihail's wife, celebrate the Jewish holidays together, bear his children. My love for him overflowed my eyes, and I dashed away tears as he continued smoking, oblivious and deep in his own thoughts.

When I returned to the kitchen. Mama's eyes were dancing with conspiratorial glee. Mama stood beside the maid, washing and putting away dishes, overseeing the cleanup.

"Mama," I told her, "go sit with your guests. I'll take care of the kitchen."

She put her arms around me. "My little girl. You're in love. I can see it."

I embraced her. "Would it be so impossible . . . to be his wife?"

Mama laughed indulgently. "In my day perhaps, but you're far too young to think of marriage in this modern world. Besides, what about medical school?" She looked into my eyes. "Be careful, my darling. I know how strong a young girl's feelings can be. But Mihail is a man . . . Even against his own best intentions, he might try to . . . well . . . take advantage . . ."

I almost laughed but caught myself in time and protested.

"Now Papa and I know a thing or two," Mama continued. "It's why we keep a close eye on you when he's here. You, my darling, have been very sheltered, despite all your racy novels. Being with a man is different from what you read."

I turned my head, my face must have been a canvas of conflicting emotions: shame, humor, confusion.

"And Mihail for a husband, I just don't know. His family is so sacrilegious. I heard the only holiday they celebrate is Communist May Day. Neither he nor his brother were bar mitzvah'ed. For all I know he is not even circumcised."

I started to assure her that he was, before I stopped myself and turned away, my shoulders shaking with laughter. Fortunately Mama interpreted my laughter as innocent embarrassment.

"Everyone says those boys in his family are *vildeh chai-yeh*. Wild animals. Brilliant, but not the best husband material." I could not look Mama in the face. "Oh sweetheart,

I've embarrassed you, speaking so frankly. Don't worry, there's a time for all this, love, marriage, children. You're still so young. There'll be time. . . ."

There Was No Time

UNDER THE 1939 Nazi-Soviet non-aggression pact, our town had been under the dominion of the Russians. But now that Hitler had attacked Russia, the Germans were on the move. In mere days, Yedinitz was retaken by the Germans and their Romanian allies.

Think of our poor town on this very early morning, July 5, 1941, the shops still closed, the streets deserted. Slowly, far in the distance, ominous shapes were moving.

I lay in an uneasy sleep. But suddenly, a dog began to bark and would not stop. Finally, I opened my eyes and rose. I peered out my window and saw nothing. I stretched and yawned.

As I stood at the window, barely awake, my mother and father suddenly burst into my room, wild with fright.

"Daniela, get dressed!" Mama said. "The Germans are here. And the Romanian Iron Guard. They're killing people right now. Dear God, help us."

My father was wrenching clothes out of my bureau and closet. "Didn't you hear your mother?" he shouted. "Get dressed! Now!"

Jacob, sleepy in pajamas, entered my bedroom, and Papa took him away to his room, leaving Mama and me alone.

"Mama, what are we to do?"

Mama closed her eyes, searching her mind for the answer. Then she opened them, suddenly strong and in control. "We . . . are going to get dressed and . . . leave. Leave this place. Now."

"To go where?"

"Papa says we have to get to Russia. Just hurry up. Where is a suitcase? Take only what you absolutely need."

She departed. I looked around my room, my eyes and head spinning. Quickly, I began to dress. I pulled off my nightgown and caught sight of my naked body in the wall mirror. This was to be the end of my lovemaking and delight. This very body might be a corpse by the end of the day—or worse than a corpse.

The Bucharest radio was blaring, "The Holy War has started against the Jews and the Bolsheviks." Yet the Russians were still insisting that "No enemy will dare to put a foot in the soil of the Soviet Fatherland. . . . There's nothing to fear from the German-Romanian capturers."

But only a few hours after this announcement we discovered that the Soviet powers and all officers were gone. Around 11:00 A.M. the Russians began to draw back to the Dniester River, the border with Russia. Shots began to be heard. At the edge of our *shtetl* bombs started to fall. We were now at the mercy of the Romanians and Germans.

After a few hours of bombardment, "to soften up the ground," the Romanians were back. Stories were beginning to go around town, each surpassing the other in horror. A Romanian cavalry unit armed with a machine gun was shooting into houses and yards. The local fascists and thugs actually welcomed them with traditional bread and salt. But for Jews, only a bullet in the head awaited.

Hitler was on the march, and he expected Romania to be an important ally in his war with Russia. We heard later how the Nazis and Romanian Iron Guard herded groups of Jewish men to the edge of a pit and began shooting as they begged for mercy, tried to run, and struggled. As a joke they hung some of the bodies from meat hooks in the municipal slaughterhouse, in the cold, concrete silence. Written in chalk across the dark coats of the dead were the words Kosher Beef.

Now many people locked themselves indoors or ran to look for family members, to at least be together at this dreadful time. Shooting, looting, and terrorizing went on day after day. I heard that the bodies of dead Jews remained on the streets and were later loaded on carts and taken away for burial.

Suddenly there was a loud banging at the door. The bell rang over and over. Dressed, I flew down the stairs and looked outside. It was Philippa! With a cry I flung open the door, and she and I embraced desperately. My mother and father rushed into the front room and cried out with relief when they saw her. Philippa was terrified, her hair down and uncombed. Even disheveled by terror at this desperate moment, I noticed how beautiful she looked, like the heroine in some Byronic romance.

When she saw our family together, Philippa began to cry. "The peasants have been mobilized to dig graves for the Jews!" she cried. My mother gasped and nearly fell to the floor. "The countess is leaving right now for London with the children," Philippa yelled at me. "The car is waiting." She turned to Mama and Papa. "We can get Daniela out if she comes with me now." She turned to me and grabbed my hands fiercely. "Come on. We have no time."

"How is it possible?" Mama said, "You can save my children?"

"The count is one of Antonescu's hunting buddies," Philippa said nervously. I noticed that she looked quickly at Jacob. "And . . . and Antonescu is still in power. He wishes to be considered a friend to the English. So he is letting us leave. But make no mistake. By tonight, this entire town will be a bloodbath."

"Oh my God!" Mama could no longer stand but sank to her knees on the floor. I rushed to embrace her and raise her up.

Philippa turned to me again. "You're dressed. Come now." She threw open the door. Outside, a car that the countess used for her visits was waiting with the engine running. Philippa had taken it and driven to get me. "This is the runabout. The Daimler is back at the estate. They're loading it down. I'm telling you, there won't be room unless you leave now."

"But my family?" I gasped out.

"We can't wait! Not another minute!" Philippa shouted.

"Daniela," Mama said, "I . . . order you to go. And take Jacob." She thrust my little brother forward. Jacob stood before Philippa, holding his violin case.

Philippa looked away. "The countess says only Daniela can come. I'm so sorry."

Jacob stood firmly before her. "I . . . won't leave Mama and Papa anyway," he said.

Philippa grabbed me. "We can get you to London. Then you can . . . bring over your family."

I swayed, overwhelmed.

"Go now. With my blessing," Papa said.

"And mine," chorused Mama and Jacob. "Please."

"Where is Mihail?" I hissed to Philippa.

"What? Mihail!" said Mama. "There is no time to think of him now!"

"The partisans came and got him last night," Philippa said. "There's fighting all over Romania. Daniela, *now*! Before they get here." Philippa grabbed my arm again.

I turned slowly and looked at my family. Then I wrenched my arm from Philippa's grasp.

"Thank you, my dearest, dearest friend. But I cannot leave my family."

Philippa grabbed me again and tried to pull me toward the door. "I do just fine without *my* family!" she hissed to me. "You little fool! They'll rape you, and then they'll shoot you. You can't save anybody." She turned to Mama. "Is that what you want for her?"

Mama cried out and shook me. They both tried to pull me through the door to drag me outside, but by now I had found my strength and had planted my feet. I fought them, holding onto the door jamb with all my strength.

"This town is doomed!" Philippa shouted in my face. "Do you doubt it?"

I shook my head. "No, I don't."

Philippa put her face close to mine. "Do you love Mihail? Do you want to live for him?" She turned to Mama and Papa. "He is her lover. Yes! They are lovers!"

"Philippa, stop," said Papa. "You don't need to tell us. We know everything." I gasped, but Papa would not meet my eyes.

"Go," I told Philippa. "You're only tormenting us now. I have made my decision. Thank you for trying to take me. I will never forget your kindness risking your life to save . . . us."

"What do you think the Iron Guard will do? The Nazis! Oh, you fool, you little fool!" Philippa screeched at me. Again, she took me by the shoulders. "Daniela, I love you," she sobbed. "I don't want you to die."

"I won't die," I told her with a calm and confidence that I did not feel. "Goodbye, Philippa. We'll see each other again, in better times. I . . . promise."

Philippa's shoulders drooped as she wept angry tears. "Mihail . . . told me that he will find you," she said. "He will come for you. He doesn't know when."

"Then he will," I said calmly. With a cry, Philippa turned and slammed the door behind her.

Now my family and I threw our arms around each other and embraced fiercely. As we tried to comfort one another, the house suddenly shook with a nearby artillery shell.

As if to put a bookend to all our hope, the noise began then and did not stop. Mama screamed and trembled. But I squared my shoulders. "Mama, we have to pack your equipment away, or it'll be looted."

Shaking, Mama gathered herself. "Yes . . . yes. Pack my equipment. For a better day."

"And Jacob and Papa need to eat. Come, let's fix them breakfast. Then we will leave for Russia."

"Yes," said Papa, "we will eat quickly. Come," he said to Jacob. "Let's finish packing for our dash to Russia. You will need your strength." He spoke with confidence to his son, though he must have understood how hopeless our situation was.

"Yes, Papa," Jacob said. I still recall his strong, nimble

hands shaking as he embraced Papa.

"Perhaps a little music would make us feel better," Papa said. "After all, we are alive and together. It is warm, we are all still fine. Let's nourish ourselves and then we will face whatever comes." Mama was murmuring Hebrew prayers, and Papa gave her a sardonic look. Even at this extremity, he would not abandon his atheism. "Jacob. Play!"

Jacob took out his violin and began to play Schubert's beautiful "Impromptu." I can never hear that piece now without thinking of him and that last morning we were all together. As the moments passed, the music gathered strength. I opened cabinets and hauled out supplies while Mama and I cooked side by side.

But Philippa had been right. We were no sooner finished eating than a banging began again. Thinking it was Philippa returning, I opened the door right away and saw to my horror a young German soldier. I gasped, and he too must have been surprised at the unexpected sight of me. He stammered for a moment, and his mouth fell open. I recoiled in terror, and Papa pushed past me to confront him.

"This is my home. Who are you?" he asked in German. The soldier looked at him in shock, as if an animal had suddenly reared up on its hind legs and spoken. He began slowly to ease his handgun out of its holster.

"*Er spricht Deutsch!*" He speaks German, the young man tossed back over his shoulder. "We are Einsatzkommando D attached to the 11th German Army," he replied.

"He speak German like a Jew," said another soldier. "But at least somebody in this godforsaken country speaks a civilized language. The Romanians are beasts.

No better than pigs."

"We're here to make this region *Judenrein*—clean of Jews," said the first German. "Are you a Jew, old man?" He grinned at Papa, who never flinched. "Not a coward anyway," laughed the German and holstered his gun. "Plenty of time later to make a mess."

Behind these Germans more soldiers had gathered to peek inside. Doubtless they had smelled the cooking food.

"*Guten Tag*," said another to Mama. "We thought perhaps you might have something for us to eat." Without pausing for an answer, he threw the door wide, and at least twenty soldiers burst in and spread throughout the house in their heavy boots, their weapons clashing and clanking. They forgot about Papa in their eagerness and curiosity.

At first many ignored us and headed for the kitchen, where they grabbed our food and began to feed. They found the wine and liquor in the living room cabinet, passing it around. They sprawled on the furniture, eating and drinking, dropping dishes and tossing half-eaten food onto the floor. Meanwhile, we huddled in a corner trying to make ourselves invisible as yet more soldiers surged through the house looking for valuables. They were in a jovial mood, especially after they got into the liquor.

One very young man addressed Mama, looking ashamed. "I . . . I apologize for my comrades," he said to her in German. "I was not raised this way. We have been fighting. We have seen our friends killed."

Mama, terrorized, did not reply but only nodded slightly.

"Someday," said the German, "all this will be over, and

we will have peace again. Console yourself."

"You are a credit to your family," Papa said.

"Shut up, old Jew," sneered another soldier. "This war is all on account of you and your puppet Roosevelt. Do we care what you think of us? You are a walking corpse."

"You were playing the Schubert impromptu, *nicht var*?" shouted another German at little Jacob. "You're not bad for a child! We heard you from the street."

I knew that I would not go unnoticed for long. The soldiers began to gather around, leering at me appreciatively. When Mama saw this, I thought she would die of fright. One soldier reached out at last and pinched my neck. He dropped his hand and felt my breasts as if he were assessing an animal or a piece of meat.

"Perfectly ripe!" he said, and the others laughed. "She won't last."

"Old Jew!" said another German to Papa. "You are rich. Where is your cash? Show us and save us time." Papa beckoned them into the bedroom, where he and Mama had stashed money in case we were ever robbed, so that the criminals would not take out their empty-handed frustration on us.

The Germans were shocked to see all of the American greenbacks that my parents had bought with their Romanian money. Mama had said that if our economy ever collapsed, American money would always have value.

"Look at all they have," said a German. "This house is stuffed with treasure. And we got here first!"

"My wife is a dressmaker," said Papa. "She serves the local countess." He wanted to let them know that they were accountable to somebody in power.

"You make dresses?" said the very young soldier who

had first spoken politely to Mama. "My mother runs a dress shop in Munich. Perhaps you could send her dresses to sell someday."

Mama nodded, her face strained with trying to smile. But she was drooping with terror.

Suddenly, a soldier had had enough of these niceties. He rose from the table and grabbed me. "Somebody has to be the first," he said to the others. They all laughed and made crude jokes as he tried to kiss me and felt my body up and down. Mama shrieked, and another German slugged her as casually as if swatting a fly. Jacob screamed at that, and Papa rushed over to protect him. He was immediately beaten and kicked. But the Germans were not really enthusiastic in their abuse. They were more interested in the food, the liquor and, of course, in me.

"Play, little Jew bastard!" said a German soldier. Jacob began to cry, his hands shaking on the violin. The soldiers were disgusted. One drew his gun and pointed it at Papa's head.

"Play—or your father dies," he said, gesturing to the violin.

"Oh leave off, Heinz," said a drunk German. "We're trying to have a good time here. You want to go back and fight some more? You'll have that soon enough."

To my horror, even more soldiers now entered; the house resonated with their harsh guttural talk and the clash of their weapons. Their foreign odors filled the air. They ran upstairs and came down dragging blankets and pillows.

"Come on, you," said the German who still held me fast. "Time to have some fun before the others find out how much you love me!" He laughed and hauled me out of the front room. I tried to wriggle free, but he held me as if I were an animal.

"Why you little vixen, are you teasing me?" He slapped my face, hard, dragged me into Papa's study, and threw me across his desk. The papers and books went flying. I saw the open *Communist Manifesto* flop onto the floor like a dead bird. From the corner of my eye I could see Papa's letter opener, and I tried to reach for it, but the soldier saw it first and grabbed it and held it close to my eye.

"I suggest you cooperate, my little beauty, and show me a good time, or I will cut up your face, and then nobody will want you."

Horror flooded through me. I belonged only to Mihail! And now this monster was going to defile me. Mihail would never want to touch me again. But there was no time to think of such things.

The soldier inserted himself and grunted with pleasure. I tried to imagine myself far away, to discard and exit my body and to pay no attention to what was happening to it. I saw at the door other soldiers, all of them shedding their coats, getting ready to take their turn. Shouting and cheering erupted; they babbled excitedly to each other and massaged themselves. So I was to be ruined. Disgraced and exposed before my mortal enemies.

I focused only on trying to survive and stay sane. I was not here. This was not me. This was not real. I thought with gratitude now that I was not a virgin, that my first experience of a man had been the best kind, the true kind. And these men were mistakes, not human beings but unnatural monsters who had crawled up from the depths of the earth onto the surface where they spread horror and violence everywhere like an infectious plague.

The soldier finished with a coarse shout and put his beefy face up against mine. "Thank you. But you should have been sweeter to me," he said. "Now I cannot protect you. But you're a fine little piece of ass, I will say that. You're no shrinking virgin, are you? You are made to give pleasure to men. Maybe you can make some money from that someday." He closed his pants and walked out while the others actually shook his hand, congratulating him for being the first.

My memories are faint now of what went on for the rest of the afternoon. They raped and hurt and defiled me in ways that I didn't know existed on the earth. All I could think of was my family suffering outside the room. At least they did not see what was being done to me. But were they still even alive? Were they being killed out in the living room while I was being repeatedly raped? Some of the soldiers were almost hesitant and gentle. I could tell that they were disgusted by this ordeal. Others though, were excited by violence and brutality. They used me as if I were nothing but a piece of meat. At last, even they became repulsed by the condition I was in.

"I wouldn't have her now," one of them said, surveying my battered body as I lay semiconscious in my agony. "She's a piece of filth."

Before I lost consciousness as they left, I wondered if I would wake up at all or if I was meant to die of this. Eventually, the pain throughout my body awakened me; I was still lying across Papa's desk. I could tell by the light outside that it must be late afternoon. All was ominously quiet. The soldiers must have moved on. I was bloodied and battered, but I knew at once that I had not been mortally wounded. My sturdy body had withstood the abuse; now if I could only keep my sanity, I could take care of my family.

Slowly, I sat up and quickly vomited. I looked around for a rag or a towel but there was none. I dragged my clothes back on. I had to get upstairs to the bathroom and try to clean myself from the filth they had left in me.

Outside, I began to hear shouting, gunfire, and explosions. I crept out of the study, and Mama roused—she had been sleeping with Jacob in her lap. At the sight of me she cried, but quietly because Jacob was still asleep. Papa turned away, weeping in deep, wrenching sobs. Jacob roused and began to cry softly in Mama's lap as she rocked him back and forth.

"Make a light in Gehenna," said Papa.

"If they see a light they'll come back," Mama said. "Or others will." She rose to come to me, but I motioned her away. I didn't want her to touch my defiled body.

"My child, let me help you," she said to me.

"Stay away, Mama," I shouted, on the edge of hysteria.

"I—"

"Leave me alone! I must clean myself."

In the light coming through the window, I tried to cover myself with my torn clothes. I limped from the room and past my family.

"We're trapped here like rats," Papa said. "We must leave and get to Russia. That's the only hope we have now."

"Schmuel," said Mama, using Papa's Yiddish name, "take Jacob and go now. Just run."

"What about you and Daniela? No, we have to stay together, no matter what. We must leave soon. Grab whatever food is left. We'll head north now, into Russia."

There was a tapping at the door. My parents looked at each other in terror. Softly Mama rose and listened at the door.

"Who is there?"

"Mrs. Mielstone, it's Priva."

"Priva! Come in. Come in." Mama opened the door, and Priva stumbled in, disheveled, her face swollen from crying.

"They shot my parents. My sister ran off with her boyfriend. I'm alone."

Mama embraced her, but I waved her away. I couldn't go near her in my state.

"Evil is unleashed," Mama said.

"Daniela . . . what have they done to you?"

Mama shook her head. "Soldiers." Priva cried, and Mama buried her face in her hands.

"They're gathering everybody tomorrow," Priva said, "and they're going to kill all the old people. The rest, they're taking to work camps."

"Oh God. This horror is just the beginning." They embraced and cried more. What else was there to do?

I crept upstairs and ran water into the bathtub. I tried to climb in and couldn't bear the pain at first. I tried again, gingerly lowering myself, muffling my cries and groans.

"Don't think," I told myself, "Just do. Don't think, just do." Slowly, I sat in the tub and closed my eyes in agony. "Stop thinking. Stop thinking. Stop stop stop!" I pounded my fist onto the tub, crying with anguish and disgust. It suddenly occurred to me: What if I was pregnant by one of those animals? Would I have the strength to kill myself? I scrubbed my raw, bruised private parts, trying not to think of my body as my own. It was just a lump of flesh that had to be purged of filth. At last I dried myself and put on the black dress that I wore to funerals.

Downstairs, I heard Mama and Priva sobbing. Suddenly the front door crashed open again. Peeking from the landing, I saw more soldiers burst in. "The Krauts got here first," one of them said in Romanian and cursed. The Iron Guard had arrived. I was to be raped again. I knew that I would not survive that. And as much as I feared and loathed the Nazis, I feared the Iron Guard more. This was truly, finally the end. No hope was left.

"Vocek, you're on guard duty," one of them said. "I'll go see if those Krauts left anything for us, the pigs." His eye fell on Priva. "Come on, Jew girl," he said and grabbed her by the hair. She screamed and as my family started forward, he said to them, "Shut up or die." He clubbed Papa with the butt of his gun. Then he pointed the gun at Jacob as Mama collapsed onto her knees. He hauled Priva screaming and pleading out the front door. More Iron Guard emerged from the kitchen, their arms full of food. I remained in the bathroom hiding behind the door, praying that they would not come upstairs.

"There's not much. No liquor at all. Those Krauts went through here like locusts. We were lucky to get this. And the girl, of course. We'll come back later. Let's go have some fun." They crowded out the front door, and suddenly we were alone.

"Priva. Dear God, no!" said Mama. "Oh God, take her before this happens to her. Let her die quickly." She threw herself to the floor and lay sobbing and beating her fists.

Papa wiped the blood from his head. "Don't tell Daniela," he said. But of course I had seen it all.

The soldiers did not come back that night. We were

left in some solitude to pack. But we didn't dare emerge from the house with the town full of soldiers. We would be shot immediately.

Days of Blood,
Days of Plunder

TWO DAYS PASSED while the Romanians and SS terrorized the town, killing people right and left, and looting everything they could. Our once lively village became a dismal ghetto, a locus of death. The homeless wandered in shock amid the rubble. Heavily armed Iron Guard were everywhere, shooting and beating.

Our goal was to join the Jews trying to cross the bridge over the Dniester River, the border with Russia. But we heard later that people escaping ran into others running back from the opposite direction. The bridge over the Dniester had been bombed, and German parachutists had already landed in Mohilev, the city on the other side of the bridge. I looked out the window and saw that they were now putting up barbed wire to keep people from fleeing. So we were trapped in Yedinitz; it was too late to get away. There was no chance at all of reaching Russia. Advance German patrols were killing the fleeing people who had run away from Yedinitz in order to save themselves—from the Germans. All roads leading to Yedinitz had been cut off.

The Romanian leader gave his followers a speech urging them to take revenge on the Jews, particularly on the Communists, for siding with the Russians against the Romanians. He said that it was the Jews' fault that the Bolsheviks had come into Yedinitz, and that the Jews had welcomed the Reds with open arms. Now they must pay dearly for their disloyalty.

A day later, all surviving Jews were ordered to gather in a central place for an "important announcement." But even at the risk of being shot, we remained in our home, barricaded now with our remaining furniture—as if that could keep soldiers out! We heard later that those who appeared at the gathering were arrested and taken away.

The gentile townspeople we had lived with in peace for generations were now ordered to loot and steal Jewish property; they could take whatever they wanted and fight it out with each other as to who got what. This madness triggered battles for each Jewish family's best possessions—heirloom dishes and glassware and sheets and handmade valuables from trousseaus. Clothing was for anybody to grab: take whatever you wanted was the order of the day. It was open season on the Jews. Jewish houses were smashed, looted, and burned, possessions—heirlooms and family records—destroyed just for the pleasure of harming and hurting their owners.

If there is any defense for some people, we did learn that if Christian villagers disobeyed that order or were found showing mercy to a Jew, they themselves could be accused of fraternizing and punished. Some pointed out to the soldiers any Jews who had collaborated with or served the Russians when they were here. Those were singled out for the worst treatment.

Mama didn't try to hide her sewing machines and fabric now; instead, she instructed the women who came to loot us on how to operate the machines.

"Here," she said to the those who had gathered at the door, hesitating and staring about, still reticent to come in. "Let me help you choose the fabric. What sorts of clothing do you and your family need?"

They entered, and she showed them patterns and fabrics, as if they were her best customers. She treated them with dignity and courtesy, helping them choose colors and cloth, threads and buttons to match. She tried to distribute the bolts of fabric equally so that everybody got something and they wouldn't fight one another. Some of the women we knew actually apologized as they made their choices.

"You know we would not steal from you, but these are terrible times," they said to Mama, "and we need to survive, too. Winter is coming. Our children have no warm clothes."

And Mama said, "I have no bitterness toward you. We are all caught up. I hope you live through this war." Some of them cried.

She taught women how to operate the sewing machines, how to load the bobbins and thread the needles. Soon, our home filled with women. Some were even chatting and brought tea with them, which they brewed and drank from our cups while Mama taught them how to make dresses that flattered them. Because even in the midst of wartime, women, incredibly, still wanted to look good. If you had not known you were in the middle of hell, you might have even imagined that the women were all at a sewing circle together.

As a dressmaker, Mama had value, which saved us for the moment. Everybody wanted to learn her craft, her techniques. The women crowded in, and even the soldiers didn't dare interrupt. Most women behaved themselves rather than fighting and looting. They marveled at the beautiful cloth and buttons and braid and lace, the colorful threads, needles, and tools. A few fights broke out when women wanted the same item, especially the sewing machines, but Mama calmed them down and gave them alternatives. She told them that if they took turns and shared the machines with one another, then everybody would get to use them.

People now rapidly depleted her fabric and supplies; everything was eventually taken, but at least we were still alive. A weird sort of peace came over the echoing rooms as people emptied them, almost as if they were moving us to another place—as indeed they were—to oblivion.

Some thanked Mama and treated her kindly. One woman even brought us bread, since the soldiers had taken everything edible, not that we felt like eating. But thanks to Mama, our own fate was postponed for a few weeks; nevertheless, all the horror being visited on the Jews still awaited us. We had no illusions. Nobody could save us.

I learned later that the Romanians had ordered the villagers to set the Jewish homes on fire, but our house had been spared. Perhaps an influential family wanted to move in here when we were gone. Why burn it to the ground? Whatever happened to our home, we now faced devastation; that we knew for a certainty.

Often, as the endless hours dragged past, we heard screaming outside and shots, people shrieking and pleading. We constantly smelled smoke; a pall hung in the air, a cloud of soot, the smell of gunpowder, of burning homes.

Miraculously, our home continued to be spared even as people walked in and out at will, carrying off any remaining furniture or the odd piece of glassware or appliance that the others had missed. Papa's books, of course, were carted out into the street and burned. My clothes were carried out, the toys I had played with as a child, and of course all of Jacob's possessions went to children in the village.

Now the looting intensified as people from other villages began to pour into Yedinitz. They were like hyenas arriving at a downed wildebeest. They hauled out rugs and beds and tables. They even tried to tear up the hardwood flooring. We were most frightened for Papa. It was well known that he was a Communist, and he knew that he could have no hope. I had never loved and treasured him so much as I did then; he awaited his fate with such quiet courage, trying to comfort our family.

"It's my fault," Papa muttered. "I thought there could be equality and justice on earth for the poor. I believed that the rich would be dispossessed by our sheer numbers and have to yield back some of their wealth accumulated on the backs of the workers. How could it not happen that we would overcome centuries of injustice and all of us come to live in happy equality? I was a fool."

"Don't torture yourself, Sam," Mama said, using the Americanized version of his name.

"Of course I hate Stalin. But I didn't think such a thug and a liar represented the pure ideals of Communism. Stalin ruined Communism, destroyed the dream. The corrupt Communists were no better than the Tsar's secret police and henchmen."

I tried to comfort him. "Dear Papa, don't blame yourself for the evil that people do. You are not at fault. It's the viciousness deep in the darkness of human nature, the madness . . . And no matter what our politics and beliefs are, we are still just Jews to them; there is no political philosophy on earth that could stop this hate and murder now."

And still Jacob managed to hang onto his violin. I kept expecting it to be ripped from his hands or smashed just for the sheer joy of destroying something valuable. Nobody in our town could play it, and it wouldn't generate much heat if burned so it survived. But perhaps the miracle of a child prodigy and the beauty of Jacob's music touched even the wicked souls of the soldiers.

Some of them who liked to show off their culture would shout to him, "Little Jew, play me some Bach," as if he were a slave for their amusement. But Jacob never complained. He would always play, with tears running down his face; he played for our very lives.

In two days, we heard that hundreds, thousands of Jews had been murdered. When would it be our turn? People were herded out of town to be shot and buried in mass graves—buried by other Jews. When they finished the burial, they themselves were killed and added to the pile of bodies. Jews were not allowed to go to the market or have any further contact with the Christian population.

With every day, the murders, robberies, arrests, and atrocities worsened. A "commission" had been set up to identify Communists and Russian collaborators. But all they really did was draw lots. If a Jew had a number "One" that meant they were a Communist and were to be shot. A number "Two" meant being spared for another day or put on burial detail. Jews on burial detail often found their own family members among the dead to be buried.

The town center became overcrowded with people, old and young, sick and well, men and women. We kept waiting to be evicted and our house burned, but time passed and nobody came for us. Perhaps people had put in a good word because of Mama's kindness to the women who looted us.

We had almost no furniture by now, but even to remain with a roof over our heads for another three weeks was a miracle. Mama went out and looked for food, but Jacob and I were not allowed on the street. Every moment we expected to lose Papa.

It wasn't only the soldiers who were doing the killing. Some locals joined in enthusiastically, though few of them had guns. But under the leadership of Romanian and Nazi soldiers, they armed themselves with butcher knives, axes, scythes, rods, and sticks. They competed with one another to tally up the greatest numbers of dead Jews.

You would never have imagined that people could be so bloodthirsty. One workman excelled in murder—I had even seen him in town many times, fixing and installing electrical devices; his cart and tools drawn by his mule were a familiar sight. He spoke Yiddish to his customers though he was a gentile. Now he turned into the bloodthirsty monster he had always been. He raped the daughters of his customers before their eyes. He had been storing up hatred for the Jews during all these years.

Yedinitz was to set an example—a standard for those that followed—in the speed, viciousness, and totality of destruction. In just three days, the Iron Guard and Nazis had slaughtered a third of our village; people of all ages, men and women, boys and girls. You could hear the shouts and orders of the murderers, and then the firing of guns, the thuds of clubs striking bodies. The crying, wailing, and pleading of the dying Jews drove us to the brink of madness.

We found out that four gallows were discovered—for a mother and her three daughters who had been tortured all night in front of the father of the family. As a result, they wanted to live no longer. Mama had known and loved that family; they had harmed no one. They had lived only for their children, educating and loving them, just the way we had.

An Appetite for Death

AT LAST THE DAY CAME when soldiers herded us out of our home with the few possessions we had held onto. Oddly, I almost felt glad to be freed of those eternal walls. They closed me in with the outrages and agony I had experienced. When I walked outside, I was amazed to see that it was a beautiful day. The summery air, clear from recent rains, literally sparkled in the sunshine, just as if the horrors had not taken place. If you looked up, you saw beauty and serenity. When you looked down at the earth, you saw such bloodshed that you could lose your sanity forever.

They herded us to the courtyard of the synagogue, and we joined the confused, frightened people milling around. We saw some that we knew and greeted them with hugs, the last we would ever have the chance to give. All the talk was of when we would be killed.

Some pretended to have hope; they boasted that they were strong and resourceful. Why would the Nazis want to kill vigorous, skilled people who could work for them?

As if drawn, I felt an urge to wander away from my family for a moment, and I saw a bundle of rags huddled in a doorway within an alley. It was my darling Priva, still alive—but as I got closer I saw that it would not be for long.

"Priva! My God. It's Daniela."

Priva looked blankly at me as I knelt beside her. "Daniela? I am dead. I am not alive anymore. I am one of the lucky ones. I'll go soon." She smiled, and I saw only bleeding gums. All of her beautiful white teeth had been knocked out.

"See what they did to me?" she said, showing me her bruised arms and her neck. She pulled up her skirt, and I turned my head.

"But why did they leave me alive like this?" she sobbed. "Why did they not finish the job and kill me quickly with a shot? I am jealous of the dead."

"Priva, come join us. We'll take care of you."

"You can't take care of me. Oh, Daniela, you are so strong. Live for me!" she cried. "Survive this war and . . . go to Palestine and raise a family. Name one of your children Priva. That would make me so happy."

I tried to pick her up and carry her out into the yard. She weighed almost nothing. I didn't know how long she had been lying there or when she had last eaten or drunk any water.

"Leave me," Priva commanded in a hoarse whisper.

"I will never leave you."

Somehow, I pulled her to her feet and kissed her sunken cheek. She gathered the strength to shuffle, moaning as I supported her through the crowded street. People withdrew in horror when they saw us.

Earlier that morning, they had separated the men from the women. I could still see Papa among the group of men, and he could see us. That was a bit of comfort. But Papa by now was in terrible shape, his beard overgrown, his eyes blank with fear and suffering. He looked around and saw other men fussing with their belongings, some arguing.

"Jews!" Papa shouted. "Don't bother with your silly belongings. We are dead men. They are going to kill us all." The others moved away from him as if he were diseased or insane.

"Communist!" a man shouted at Papa. "You don't know any more than the rest of us."

Papa turned away bitterly. A middle-aged man ran up to Papa. I recognized him as a shopkeeper; he had been a rotund, cheerful fellow, but now he was gaunt and his plump face had deflated, sagging with grief.

"Moshe!" Papa reached out and the two embraced. "How is your family, my friend?"

Moshe shook his head. "They took away Ida and the children." He shrugged. "We ran at first, we thought we could get to Russia, but we got only a few miles. They found us, and they shot so many. May the murderers all drown in the blood of their victims. I hear we men are going to be deported now to Transnistria, across the Dniester, to work. There's a tire factory there . . . or is it shoes? I know something of cobbling. . . ."

"My old friend," said Papa, "we had a few good times, didn't we?"

Moshe cried in racking sobs. "I could die with a happy heart if I only knew my family was safe."

Papa thought of something. "My daughter's tutor, Mihail Borowiak? Any news of him?"

"Oh them!" Moshe said. "They were all armed to the teeth when the Germans showed up. They blew up two cars and shot some soldiers."

I saw Papa laugh. "Ha ha! So he did what he said after all. He was right, and I was wrong. Were they all killed then?"

My heart began pounding so hard I thought I would faint.

"No," said Moshe, "they escaped in the melée. But the Germans shot so many in revenge...."

"They would have shot them anyway," Papa said. "They have done nothing but kill people."

As they spoke, a couple of large vans pulled up to the gates of the compound in front of the synagogue.

"This is it," said Moshe, "our transport to the work camps. Why not be optimistic? They need strong men." Iron Guard and Nazi troops begin shoving men toward the vans. Prodded by machine guns, the men stumbled up the ramps. Papa waved to us as Mama wept into her shawl. One man hesitated and was shot dead on the spot.

"A lucky one," Papa said.

"Stay with me, Schmuel," Moshe said to Papa. "We'll work as a team. Together we can ..."

Papa put his arm around his friend. "Yes, Moshe. Together. Always." Moshe began to mutter his prayers as they lined up. After a moment, Papa, to my amazement, joined him in the ancient Hebrew words. I knew that he did it to comfort his friend. And that was my last memory of Papa. My last vision.

I heard much later that they were taken to a clearing. One man, a Christian who had been dragged along to help the Nazis commit their murder, had survived the war. He was able to tell me what happened to Papa and the other men from Yedinitz on that day, how my father died. This is what he told me:

"The vans, loaded with their human cargo, came to a stop and parked, idling with their engines running on the outskirts of the forest that surrounded our town. Three Nazi soldiers immediately descended on them, running pipes from the engines into the crowded vans. They were showing the Iron Guard how to kill people efficiently with carbon monoxide. As the exhaust began to fill the vans, shouting and pounding erupted, shaking the sides of the vans.

"Inside the truck's cab, the fat, mindless driver sat looking out the window, smoking a cigarette while the men inside the van died. He tossed the cigarette away, bored. Then he picked up an apple. As the men begged for air, he sat and munched his fruit. He pressed down the gas pedal and revved the engine to send more exhaust into the van.

"Suddenly," said my informer, "his head exploded. Blood spattered the windshield. In the other van, the cab burst into flames from a grenade. The shrieking driver, on fire, pulled himself out, his leg blown off.

"Partisans, Mihail among them, swarmed into the clearing, shot the three Nazi soldiers, and bashed open the doors of the two vans. The prisoners inside spilled out, gasping, some were unconscious and many had already died.

"The partisans quickly waded among the prisoners," the man told me. "They grabbed the stronger, living men, dragged them to their feet, pounded their backs, and gave them water. Your father and Moshe were already dead in one another's arms. Mihail had paused for a moment and looked at your father. Then he reached down and closed his and Moshe's eyes. Another partisan was shooting those who were dying, gasping out bloody froth, and suffering. There would be no saving them—only a quick death could end their agony.

"One of the partisans shouted, 'Mihail! Get your ass out of there!'

"Mihail gestured to your father and said, 'I knew this man.'

"'You'll know your maker in a minute,' said the partisan. 'Come on!'

"'He was to be my father-in-law,' said Mihail. 'We were too late.'"

My informer had tears in his eyes as he continued the story. "'Only by a minute or two,' the partisan said before adding, 'We'll get better.' I remember him grinning jovially with missing teeth. 'It was a good raid,' he tried to assure Mihail. 'Five pigs dead, and we gained a few good stout fellows.'

"I remember Mihail smiling grimly, before responding, 'If only I'd been able to save the old man.'

"'Romantic!' the partisan screamed at him. 'We're not here to rescue and ride off into the sunset like a Hollywood movie. We're here to kill. It's a good day for killing Nazis and Iron Guard swine!'

"He then slapped the back of a prisoner, who had been stumbling along, dazed and coughing. 'Ho! Look sharp, you lucky man,' the partisan yelled at the poor fellow. 'You're going to kill some Nazis before you die!' He laughed again with his broken fangs as they trudged into the woods and disappeared."

Now that Papa was gone, we were truly without hope of escape. The synagogue yard had become a wasteland of makeshift tents and lean-tos. Most women and children simply sat on the ground, too weak to move. Mama, Jacob, Priva, and I huddled together.

"Mama, I still have some food," Jacob said, gesturing to Priva.

"Give her," I said. "Give her."

Mama said to me, "Yes, but we have to save some for ourselves, too. People are wolves here, God help them." But suddenly Mama leaned closer to Priva. "She's gone, the angel."

"You're only saying that!" I shouted at Mama, my face contorted with grief. Until that moment I had thought that perhaps Priva could survive and recover. But Mama cried out, "Please, Daniela. I would never lie to you." I embraced Priva, thinking of our last trip to the bookstore, how lovely she had been and how hopeful she was that life would hold some romance for her.

But our suffering had only begun. An Iron Guard soldier now paused at the sight of Jacob. He was a lusty, cruel-looking young man, his prominent eyes pale blue. His lips were gross, thick and red, shiny with spittle.

"What's this little shit doing here? He belongs with the men." He turned to Jacob. "Don't you want to be a man, little piglet?" He laughed coarsely.

"Please!" Mama begged the soldier. "He's a little boy. He's nine."

"A boy, ha! Let's see if he's a man yet." He yanked down Jacob's pants as other Iron Guard soldiers gathered to laugh.

"Just as I thought. Circumcised. A pussy, like a girl. Come here, you boy-girl. I fancy a little tender meat."

He grabbed Jacob and kicked away Jacob's violin case. Mama ran up and grabbed the soldier's arms.

"Please! Please! He's a child. I beg you. You have a mother."

"Don't talk about my mother, Jew whore!"

I came running up as the soldier bashed Mama's face with the butt of his gun. When Mama picked herself up and went at him again, bleeding, the soldier casually shot her in the chest with his handgun. She staggered backward into my arms.

Jacob and I screamed, "Mama!" "Mama!" Mama looked at us; her eyes were glazed, unknowing already. The stunned crowd screamed in horror and turned away. Mama began to cough blood, choking. People started forward to try to help her and were restrained by others.

"Oh for Jesus' sake," said her murderer, "can't a man get a little peace and quiet around here?"

He noticed me holding Mama. "Heyyy . . . Have we met before, darling?" He turned away from Jacob. As I stooped to grab my brother, the soldier casually shot him in the head. Shrieking and wailing, I was dragged away by another Iron Guard.

"Now don't give me any trouble or you'll meet the same fate," said one of them. The soldiers gathered around, some laughing. But I noticed that one or two were actually taken aback by this psychopathic viciousness. They knew their comrades were criminal beasts.

"Who ever thought we'd find a pretty one here among these Raggedy Anns?" said a soldier, looking at me appreciatively. "Hold still, you. I don't want to spoil your pretty face. You're meant for better things than to be wasted on the pavement here." To the others he said, "You see what a nice fellow I am?"

He actually started to open up his pants right there in

public as I struggled. My grief and fright were stimulating his lust. He could not wait to have me. The other soldiers laughed, but one German SS Guard assigned to the Romanian detail was plainly uncomfortable.

"Leave off," he said to the solders. "You Iron Guard are a bit much."

The soldier who held me laughed. "What? Why, you German aristocrat, you. You come here and try to tell us how to treat a Jewess? We tell *you* how to treat a Jewess."

The soldiers gathered around, laughing. They resented the Nazis for looking down on them as animals—as indeed they did.

The SS soldier was offended. "You're barbarians. No, I mean it. You are! Right in public, you mate like an animal? Do you shit in public, too?"

"Shut up, you German prince," said the Iron Guard soldier.

"I was raised in a decent home," said the German. "Take her out of my sight. I don't want to see your ugly ass! What a pervert you are!"

The Iron Guard soldier, drunk and full of lust, smacked my rear and pretended to saunter as he hauled me away. Now the soldiers laughed even harder.

As I was dragged to my fate, I heard people chanting the Jewish prayer, "*Sh'ma Yisrael.*" It rang in my ears, and I chanted it myself.

Transnistria: Hiking to Hell

WORDS CANNOT SUFFICE to describe what took place, so I will simply say that in 1930, there were about 207,000 Jews in our region. In 1942, there were two hundred twenty-seven miserable souls left alive. To my dismay, I was one of them.

By now the weather was changing. The once blue sky clouded over and began to dump freezing rain on the hapless victims below. The Romanian guards were always ready to beat, shoot, and rape. I became inured to their abuse. We were marching eastward. I knew that I would not survive this, and I welcomed death whenever it would arrive to set me free.

Our meager supplies of food had run out, and people were starving in front of my eyes. Sometimes the soldiers tossed me their leftovers, which I tried to share, but if they caught me giving food away they shot the intended recipient. Some people resented me for being the soldiers' sex slave; they thought I was a willing participant in their horrors. So I was denied even the comfort of my own people. I was less than an animal.

I found myself trudging along a country road outside Yedinitz. Ironically, it was an extension of the very road

I used to take on my bicycle to the count's estate where I had met Mihail for our luxurious days of sensuality and pleasure. How I was being punished for the hours we enjoyed.

Nazi and Romanian motorized and foot troops zipped up and down this dusty, littered highway herding a long column of suffering Jews. Children wandered without parents. People were frequently shot and thrown into a ditch on the side of the road. Peasants stalked our column and pounced to rob the bodies of the dead or grab the possessions of the living.

Stumbling along, I learned that we were being deported to an area between the Dniester and Bug Rivers known as "Transnistria." The Germans were pulling out and had handed control of that area to the Romanians through one of their cozy little pacts. But what did it matter who pulled the trigger? We were all doomed and were to suffer yet unforeseen horrors before that release.

People would go into the fields and try to gather up potatoes and beets that the harvester had missed. That was all the food we could find. At night, everyone was drenched, sitting in the muddy puddles because the rain was constant by now. People died during the night, and at first light we saw their corpses, people who had just been talking and singing and praying. We tried to dig pits and bury them at least.

We were now approaching the Dniester River. We passed a *shtetl* whose residents had managed to run away to Russia and talked about how perhaps they had made it to safety. We needed to think that some Jews at least had survived.

I was by now thin and bruised, my once glossy, wavy

hair was matted with dust, my eyes dull with suffering. Two Romanian soldiers passed and eyed me. The old feeling of dread arose, but they only looked at each other and laughed.

"That one . . . I used to fancy her," one of them said. A shudder of disgust passed through me, though I had long ago learned to see my body only as a lump of flesh that my soul was somehow trapped in.

"I wouldn't fuck her with your dick now, Radu!" The other soldier laughed. I quickened my pace a little, anxious to be out of their line of vision. But I was not to be so lucky.

"Hey you!" the soldier called after me. I turned, because if I ignored him I could be beaten. "Go take a wash in the river. Phew! You are not fit to touch."

"You want to have some fun tonight?" the other soldier called to me. "We've got vodka. Come on. We aren't so bad. Give a soldier a good time. Tomorrow we may all be dead." To make his point, he pulled out his revolver and gestured to me. People turned in their trudging and watched the scene. Some pitied me but others were envious at the attention I still attracted.

The soldiers were following me now, laughing coarsely as I tried to blend into the crowd, but one of them finally reached out and grabbed me by the hair, pulling me off my feet and onto my knees in the dirt.

"Jew whore! You snub my buddy here? Who do you think you are? You want to die right now?"

"Yes! Shoot me now!" I looked the soldier boldly in the eye, hoping that he would end my suffering right then and there. I reached out for his gun, and he let me grab it and put it to my head. The watching Jews screamed. But the soldier only wrenched the gun away, laughing.

"Phew! She stinks *and* she's crazy as a loon. You want her? You bring her." He laughed and pretended to brush me off his hands. The other soldier grabbed me by the arm and dragged me with them.

"A soldier's life is hard! What we put up with out here," he said to nobody in particular.

I saw that they were pushing and dragging me toward a large outbuilding. The Iron Guard soldiers had taken over some noble's country home. Above the door now were words in Romanian: Field Headquarters, Hotin Legion.

As the two soldiers passed, still dragging me, an attaché came out and hailed them. "Hold up, you two," he said. The soldiers stopped. Since he was not an officer, they did not salute him.

"What is it? You front office types want in on our fun now?"

"I can't believe it," said the attaché. "You've done my work for me. Saved me a trip into that smelly crowd out there."

"Glad to oblige. Now what are you talking about?" The attaché held up a picture of me in happier times and then held it up next to my face. It was me, all right, but it seemed another person entirely, a smiling, healthy face, looking confidently into the camera. This picture had been taken by Philippa on a sunny afternoon out by the fruit trees in our backyard. I had then taken the camera and snapped one of her, too. Who knew where she was now or if she was even alive?

The picture had been taken after Mihail and I had become lovers. Now, under my layer of grime, I was smiling at the thought of him.

"I said, what's your name?" The attaché was shouting, commanding of me. "Are you deaf? What's your name? Look at her smiling. She's an idiot."

"Daniela Mielstone," I said. "I am the last of my family."

"Come with me," said the attaché, which caused my two captors great consternation.

"Hey! We saw her first. We even got her cleaned up for a little party. We dipped her in the river. See?" He lifted my skirt, and when I grabbed it away he threatened me with his fist.

"Better find another," said the attaché.

"Why? She's just a Jew." The attaché gave them an ironic look.

"Come on," said the attaché and motioned me away from the puzzled soldiers. He himself recoiled as I approached and didn't touch me, which was a blessing, so I followed him obediently up the steps of the headquarters. Out in the road the soldiers were mocking and whooping.

"Wait here." The attaché left me in the front entryway. I looked around in amazement. The half-ruined house had once been elegant and comfortable, but of course it had been trashed and casually abused. Windows were cracked or broken, walls were scuffed and stained. A fire burned in a fancy fireplace that had been scorched and neglected. The turned legs of antique furniture protruded from the blaze. Broken chairs and tables that had once been elegant and borne sumptuous feasts were now stacked nearby as firewood. Sofas and armchairs were stained with beer and food.

I stood dazed and brutalized before a long dining table that was serving as a desk. Behind it sat the commanding officer—Major Dragulescu, as cruel-appearing as one would expect from somebody in his position. He was nearly bald, with slack skin, high cheekbones, and thin lips. His colorless eyes widened as he surveyed me, almost with the gaze of a connoisseur.

"Sir, I found her. This is Daniela Mielstone."

"So fast?" He continued scanning me with his lidless reptilian eyes.

"She . . . happened to be passing by."

The attaché handed the photo to the major, who held it up and compared it to me more carefully, top to bottom. He made a dismissive motion to the attaché.

"The picture is outdated . . ." the attaché tried to explain.

"But it's her, all right. Leave us now."

"Yes, Sir." The attaché clicked his heels, turned, and vanished from the front door.

The major addressed me: "This is what you used to look like, eh? You've gone downhill fast."

I turned away, unable to confront my former self. "This is what you have done to me," I spoke up, my voice cracking, not caring if he pulled out his gun and shot me.

The major suddenly lost interest in me, leaving me standing before him while he picked up a pen and began to write.

Shivering, I cautiously edged closer to the fire.

Without looking up, Major Dragulescu said, "You look like hell. But you were pretty once." I stared and said nothing. "I don't understand the aristocracy," the major continued. "They think it's still the nineteenth century." I shook my head slowly, not knowing what he was talking about.

"We are carrying out a campaign of *curatirea terenului*—the cleansing of the ground," said the major. "We are getting rid of the Jews, the cripples, the morons. The Nazis have no patience with the imperfect. They are teaching us Romanians to become more like them. This is what you have been caught up in."

I dared to raise my puzzled eyes to his.

"You've just been handed your life back, and all you can do is stand there staring like a cow?" The major rose and walked around me in a circle. "So! You were once a little diversion for Count Kányádi?"

I was speechless. I had only met the count a couple of times, and at no time had anything passed between us.

He came closer to me. "The count's English mistress has convinced him to intervene on your behalf, if you were still alive, which you appear to be. Barely."

My knees began to buckle. "Philippa," I whispered; it sounded like a name from another universe.

"What did you say, Jewess?"

"She . . ." I suddenly went numb and barely caught myself before I fell to the elegant marble floor.

"We have two problems," said the major, "which I will explain. Sit!" He commanded. "Sit down! You're wobbling."

I crept toward an armchair I saw from the corner of my eye.

"Not that one. That's a good chair. Sit there." He motioned to a wooden chair, and I sank into it and retreated like a cornered animal.

"Two issues, as I said. In the first place, we Romanians are not capable of handling so many Jews. The Germans ask too much. Tens of thousands of you arrive here half dead already—while we cannot bury the corpses we already have. The corpses are burying us!" He guffawed at his own wit.

"Secondly, did we ask for this war?" He rose and paced. "Roosevelt and his Jew financiers manipulated international politics to bring America out of its Great Depression. Yes, the Germans will lose, but do not fool yourself." He pointed his finger at me as I sat, shivering. "You Jews will all die nevertheless. And stop that shaking! You're warmer here than you've been in weeks!"

I stared numbly and tried without success to control my limbs.

"And now suddenly, you are my responsibility." He stroked his chin, calculating. "Not that I care if you die, mind you. But if I give you back to the count, I will perhaps earn myself his gratitude, a bonus. The count is still a rich man. On the other hand, if I harbor a lazy Jew, my subordinates and the troops will become resentful, and I could get demoted or worse. You see my problem?"

Slowly, I nodded. The slightest wrong move could bring a bullet. Yet how many times had I wished to die, and quickly? The human mind is a paradox.

"Anyway," the major continued, "for better or worse, here we are. So I am going to do us both a favor. I was told you were studying to be a doctor . . ." I tried to protest that I had barely begun, but he shut me up with a sharp glare. "So I am sending you to our field hospital to be a nurse. We need nurses desperately, and I cannot imagine even a Jew would be such a monster that you would purposely harm wounded soldiers."

I said nothing to this; I knew that prisoners in factories purposely sabotaged the weapons and instruments of war they were working on. Isn't a soldier an instrument of war? I wondered just how mad and warped my mind had become. How desperate for vengeance was I?

"Perhaps," the major was continuing, "if we both survive this infernal conflict, you will put in a word for me with the count, yes? In exchange for me saving your life?"

I nodded again, keeping my eyes on the floor. "He is living in London and is, as I said, a rich man. He managed to evade the worst of the war, of course. Perhaps . . ." the major was thinking aloud now, and his voice took on a timbre and relish as he envisioned himself at an advantage, "once all this is over, he will have a position of responsibility for me. On one of his estates . . . I could manage the staff. I am an excellent organizer . . . Why . . ." he actually laughed, "we might all end up as friends someday. And look back on the war only as dreadful memory—fading quickly, let us hope."

The major broke off, walked to the fire, stooped, and threw in some boards. He surveyed me, his eyes glittering. "You look better to me with a little color in your cheeks. Now," he commanded, "strip! At least you will not get chilblains on your ass!"

He began to unbutton his pants, motioning to me impatiently.

"You heard me? Or did you not? Are you ungrateful? Hm? Maybe you want to go back out there," he gestured at the door with his hand.

I shook my head.

"Show your gratitude, or I'll give you to the soldiers. If you die, I'll just tell the count you could not be found."

Slowly, I removed my tattered blouse. The major

sidled toward me, as unashamed of his nudity as if I had been a cow.

"That's better. You little minx. You Jews are all alike. First you wail and cry, but then you like it, too." He approached and felt my body all over, pressing himself against me.

"Ptu! Skin and bones. Well, it's a war, what do we expect? We take what we can find." He fumbled with my naked body, roughly pushed my legs apart, and inserted himself.

"You like me better now?" He pressed his face to mine. "I'm a powerful man. I can help you. Tell me how strong I am."

". . . a p-p-powerful man," I stammered mechanically.

"Now tell me how much you like me."

"I . . . like you," I said dully. "I . . . like . . . you."

"Say it like you mean it. I'm your darling boy, am I?" The major reached his hands up and began to choke me. "You want me to kill you?"

"Yes."

"Ah, you can't fool me. You still want to live. Maybe you want to kill me, eh? Ha ha ha!" He finished at last and hurled me away from him with a grunt. Naked, he strolled to his desk, leafed through his papers, almost forgetting I was there. I cowered near the fire, teeth chattering.

"Warming your bony flanks? We'd better get you some food." The major was in an expansive mood now, drinking brandy. "You're worse than a corpse. You're a skeleton, with all the meat gone. But what do I expect, it's wartime. What I put up with . . ."

He grinned at me. "We can be friends now, yes? Now that we are lovers. We'll get to know each other better in this hellhole." I looked at him blankly, not knowing what to do next.

"Well? What do you want, a royal chariot? Cover yourself. Oh, you're no fun at all!" He laughed and began to pull up his pants as a couple of officers stopped at the doorway.

"What is it?" he called to the men as they self-consciously tried to look anywhere but at him. "Nothing you haven't seen before. Don't bring me any more of these half-starved Jews. Give me a good, plump little. Somebody who knows how to laugh!" The officers smiled and motioned to him that they would return later and beat a retreat.

The major picked up the bottle of brandy and shoved it at me.

"Here, drink. We've got a long night ahead of us, my little tart. Maybe this will loosen you up." I tried to drink, gagged helplessly, and began to dry heave. The major came over and tipped the bottle up to my mouth. The liquor dribbled into my throat and down my face.

"Come on. Come on. Keep it down. You're wasting good booze. Lap it up like a dog!" Laughing, he pushed me to the floor and forced my head down to lick up the spills.

"All right, enough fun for now. We have to get you cleaned up and fed if you're going to warm my bed tonight."

The major shooed me through the large mansion as lounging soldiers snapped to attention and then elbowed each other, laughing when we passed.

"The officers always get the best pieces of ass," I heard one of them say.

"She was fun while she lasted," said another.

The major wheeled on the men, still jocular. "Whoever touches my little honey, I'll shoot." He strode away, and I heard the soldier say, "Who'd have his syphilitic seconds?" They laughed, their snarky voices receding. I staggered from the effects of the brandy, trying not to vomit again, and followed him up the winding stairs.

Major Dragulescu's bedroom was on an upper floor of the headquarters. He hurled me onto the bed and left. I stole a glance around and spotted a revolver lying on the bureau. I picked it up and put it into my mouth and pulled the trigger. It clicked empty.

The major saw and turned to me. "Don't play with that. I'm lucky I hadn't loaded it yet. I have no decent maid to clean up the mess." He came over and took the gun from my hand and put it back on the bedstand. In his other hand was some bread and a hunk of cheese, which he tossed to me.

"Here. Put this in your mouth instead. It'll give you energy, and you're going to need it." He laughed and began to unbutton his uniform.

The night ended at last. As the major snored beside me, I lay staring into the darkness, eyes wide. Even the unaccustomed softness of a clean bed and a pillow under my head barely registered. I thought of my family and tried in my mind to explain to them my new role as a whore. I knew that Mama would forgive me, but the pain this would cause Papa and Jacob I could not imagine.

"My little brother," I whispered, imagining him playing and cavorting, as I always did. "Jacob, you mischievous boy, on your way to becoming a splendid man. May God care for your soul. Papa, yes, I am praying to the God you denied up to your last breath to look for you among all of the millions of dead. My family, I will come join you as soon as I can. Please forgive me for being a coward and not taking my worthless, blemished life just yet." I cried quietly, afraid to wake the major and his lust again.

The Price of Survival

I AWAKENED to a gentle push; somebody was shaking my shoulder quietly so as not to rouse the major. Dawn was barely coming through the curtains of the large bedroom. I sat up with a gasp.

An elderly woman stood beside the bed. When I opened my eyes, she put a finger to her lips and motioned for me to follow her.

I sat up, covering my nakedness, but she made a gesture not to worry. She held open a robe that she had draped across her arm—maroon linen with satin trim. I shrank away, but she smiled and urged me to put it on.

The major shifted in his sleep and mumbled some unintelligible words. The softness and cleanness of the robe on my skin was almost painful; it was more than I could bear. I wrapped it around me and followed the old woman out of the bedroom.

"I'm Elizabeta," she said, studying me closely. "I wait on the major, and I'll look after you, too. The war has taken my children and my husband. I have nothing but strangers around me, so I befriend them."

"Thank you," I said. "I too have nobody . . ." I stopped myself, thinking of Mihail, and Philippa, too. Perhaps I was not as bereft as I had thought. "I will be your friend, though I'm a Jew."

"I do not hate the Jews," said Elizabeta, "although everybody else does. I don't know why. My grandchildren's doctor was a Jew. He tried to save them from typhus. They were so small . . . we had an epidemic before the war broke out. I believe he would have traded his life for theirs. My daughter committed suicide."

"I'm sorry about your family," I said.

Elizabeta dabbed at her eyes with a chapped, roughened claw. "They were beautiful children, my daughter and her babies. The best a woman could want. I give thanks that I had them as long as I did. I will tell you about them sometime. Talking about them brings them to life for me."

"I understand," I said.

"I was working on the estate here as a maid when the Germans invaded. They sent my husband to a work camp, and there he quickly died. He was sick with tuberculosis, they told me, but I know they just worked him to death."

When the Germans left to fight in Russia Elizabeta had remained to serve the Iron Guard who took their place.

She was a portly, kind-looking crone with her gray hair wrapped around her head in two thick braids. She had the wide cheekbones and sloe eyes of the Slavs, another "low" race that the Nazis intended to eradicate, just not as quickly as the Jews.

"The Nazis wanted to take our lands and starve us to death," she told me. "They needed to expand eastward and our land was in their sights. *Lebensraum*, they called it. They calculated on making slaves of us and eventually replacing us with Germans. That would be after they had killed all the Jews."

"I think they have by now killed all the Jews," I said.

"In this region they were all dead within months. I am always surprised to see Jews still alive at all in Romania and Ukraine."

"I will join the dead soon," I told her. "The sooner the better."

"Ah no," said Elizabeta, "life is God's gift, and we cannot discard it."

"How can you still believe in God after what you have seen?" I asked her.

"What else is there to believe in?" she replied. She led me to the kitchen, which was well stocked with food.

"Today you are to go to the field hospital and begin work as a nurse," she said. "It is the plan of the major that you survive and return to your friends. There is much fighting going on right now in Russia. At first the Nazis were winning, destroying everything and everyone in their path, of course. The major tells me they are now losing their momentum. They cannot take Moscow, and their supply lines are overextended. The bombing of the British and Americans is starting to take its toll. They did not learn that nobody invades Russia and returns victorious. The Russian land always triumphs over its invaders. And then it takes its revenge. Soon the Germans will have to retreat over the land that they destroyed in their frenzy, and the land will repay by starving them."

"May it happen soon," I said.

"The major tells me that the Red Army will chase the Germans west, back to where they came from, until they overrun Germany—and then they will have their vengeance."

"The Germans are beaten then?"

"Oh my, yes. The trouble is, they do not know it—or perhaps they do. Hitler doesn't appear anymore. But they will not leave off until they have killed the last of your people, and of mine if they have the bullets left. Even if they lose the war, they will take the Jews with them to perdition."

"And the Romanians?"

"They are trying to surrender to the Allies," Elizabeta told me. "They have no appetite for a losing war. But the Germans will never allow them to. So the fighting and death will continue, all in a lost cause."

This whole time Elizabeta was preparing me a breakfast, the first decent food I had had in months.

"Eat slowly, Daniela, and just a little at first. You are in a condition of starvation and your body will reject more than a few bites. It will make you sicker instead of healthy. The major wants you to be healthy when you return to your friends in London, once all this is over."

"Why can't he leave me alone? I would rather go back on the death march than share his bed."

"Shhhh. Men are beasts, Daniela. I was raped too many times to count, old as I am. If the Russians overrun us here, they will rape us for sure, since they see us as aiding the Nazis. The Russians don't care what our stories are. They are losing millions of people at the hands of the Germans and their allies. And the Romanians are their allies. That's all they have to know. Stalin has ordered the Russian soldiers to take revenge for their dead families on every enemy woman they find. Especially the Germans and Austrians."

"The Germans are losing. That gives me strength to live."

"It is the beginning of the end—but do not ever tell the major I said that. After what Hitler and his Wehrmacht did to the Russian people, the Russians will kill me as sure as the sun rises."

"I won't let them," I said, irrationally, as I was barely alive myself.

I trudged with Elizabeta to the field hospital—tents and outbuildings as far as I could see. When she brought me to the office, they gave me a clean uniform and a badge. That was how simple it was to become a nurse.

I stood at the threshold of the main building and walked inside. And then I stopped as if I had hit a wall. As much death and injury as I had seen, I had never seen anything approaching what I now confronted. As far as the eye could reach were injured men, some conscious and crying out, others moribund or already dead. They had been shot to pieces, crushed, and burned. Some didn't seem to be injured, but had simply gone mad, babbling and chanting, praying and even singing.

New arrivals were stacked up bleeding on the floor or on makeshift canvas beds in the decrepit hallways of the building. These were the lucky ones. Outside, the wounded simply lay under crude canvas tents or even on the cold ground itself.

In a moment, the head nurse descended on me with a tray of medical supplies and pointed me toward a row of beds.

"That is your ward," she said. "Find out what they need, and take care of them." She handed me a clipboard. "We are not animals here. You are to record your treatment and time of medication as best you can for the doctor. We have only two doctors to serve these many people. The other doctors are on the battlefield."

And that was the extent of my preparation. All my training was gained by experience—watching and learning from others. I paid close attention and picked up every skill I could and practiced when I found the time, learning how to clean out fragments of dirt and bone and metal and stitch a wound properly. I knew that these soldiers were my enemies, but I discovered that I could not imagine intentionally harming anyone helpless in my care.

And so I entered the medical profession after all, caring for and saving my mortal enemies, any one of whom could have been the murderer of my people or the rapist of my sweet Priva.

On that first morning, as I walked uncertainly down the row, a wounded soldier on a makeshift gurney grabbed at me.

"Nurse . . . please . . . water," he said in Romanian.

A second soldier whose wounded leg was bleeding through its bandages caught my eye. "Morphine. If you have a soul, get me morphine."

I looked at the terrible wounds and wondered how these men could even be alive. I tried not to show how hopeless I felt they were. Instead, I nodded.

"I'll see what I can do," I said. "I . . . I'll find some."

"God bless you," said the men. "You are an angel."

I looked around helplessly and spotted two nurses dressing a wound together at a bedside.

"I am Daniela," I said to them.

"Welcome. I'm Lenuta," said one; she appeared to be

in her forties with graying blonde hair and narrow eyes of no particular color. She was tough, hefty, and deeply cynical. She told me that she could not recall a time when she had not been disillusioned and bitter. The other nurse, Ileana, was in her thirties, dark and thin, not unattractive, but beaten down, as we all were.

"Please," I said, indicating the two soldiers I had just passed, "they are asking for water and . . . and morphine."

"Oh are they?" said Ileana. "Outside is a pump. Take one of those pitchers and fill it." She indicated a large white pitcher, chipped and cracked. "We have to boil our water first or it will kill them surer than Russian bullets."

I glanced helplessly at the pleading soldiers and showed them the pitcher.

"Wh-where do I boil it?"

"Outside. There's a fire. But you probably have to gather wood first. Everything here you have to do for yourself. Most of the orderlies were called to the front. Only we women are left, and the cripples of course."

". . . and the morphine?"

Ileana laughed, showing crooked, cigarette-stained teeth. "*Morphine*? Where do you think you are? Paris? New York? Morphine? Ha ha. Ask God."

I exited, clutching the pitcher but not before I heard Lenuta saying to Ileana, "That's the Jewess the major's taken a fancy to."

"A 'fancy?'" said Ileana, "He's been bragging to the men about her right and left. The old fart. I'll bet he's part Jewish."

"Not likely," said Lenuta. "My friend Stefan saw him shoot twenty of them outside Kishinev. Boom boom boom, one after the other, like they were cattle."

"Water, water, please!" shouted the men when they saw me with the pitcher.

"She's getting it," said Lenuta to the soldier. "You'll dry your mouth out shouting at us." She turned to Ileana. "Even Jewish hands are welcome here. I haven't slept in three days." The two nurses looked at each other.

"Bedpans!" They laughed in chorus. They stopped laughing at the sight of an older man who wore a blood-stained white coat.

"Daniela," called Ileana, "come back here for a minute and meet Dr. Tomescu, the best doctor in the world." I hurried to them and stood blushing while Dr. Tomescu looked me skeptically up and down. He was in his late forties, tough, cynical, and authoritarian, with a shock of black hair and blue eyes, and an embittered hurt look to him that told me that he had probably once been an idealistic physician.

"You've had a hard time, it appears," he said. I nodded. "Not much for conversation, eh? All the better. We have work to do here, as you see." He turned to the nurses, "I'm glad our wounded and dying are doing so well that nurses have time to stand around gossiping and making jokes."

"We're waiting for the Jew to fetch some water," said Ileana.

"She's the major's new bed-warmer," Lenuta said. I closed my eyes with humiliation.

"Whoever helps me save these boys is welcome in my hospital," said Dr. Tomescu, looking at me sharply. "Unlike others, I have more important things on my mind than the sex life of Major Dragulescu." He turned to me again. "You were a medical student, I'm told." I said nothing. "So let her care for patients and not just slop shit," the doctor said to Lenuta and Ileana.

"Some of them would rather die than be cared for by a Jew," said Ileana.

"If they prefer that," said Dr. Tomescu, "we'll respect their wishes." He lingered for a moment.

"Our boys are taking a beating in Russia. How could Hitler have been so stupid to invade? Didn't he ever hear of Napoleon? The whole country is one gigantic frozen trap." The nurses nodded. "And our beloved Antonescu throws in his lot with the Nazis. Our lot. *Their* blood," he said, indicating the patients. "And it's on his hands. Did he really think Hitler could win this war? Against America, too? It's madness. A waste of life."

Outside, I wandered about looking for a water source. I discovered that the pump was not working. "It's a temperamental pump," said the orderly. "It goes dry, and then you have to get your water from the river. Bring a pail." He pointed to a stack of rusty pails. "And don't forget to gather wood to feed the fire. I just brought back a load, and it's almost gone."

Two giant cauldrons were boiling bloody clothes. Orderlies poked at the clothes with long sticks, occasionally drawing out a garment. Beside the cauldrons were jugs of lye and other ingredients to make a crude detergent.

"I'll show you how to do the bedclothes," said the orderly, "after you have boiled the water. We are at high risk of typhus and cholera here, and so we have to boil everything." He showed me his arms, scalded red and pink. "This is what you have to look forward to."

At last, I re-entered with a pitcher of boiled water that I had managed to cool enough to be drinkable. When I found the bed of the soldier who had been pleading for water, a sheet had been pulled over his head.

So that was my first day. I held the hands of two men who died on my watch. Toward noon, I held the instruments while Dr. Tomescu performed an amputation of a foot. I changed bandages as best I knew how, and I learned how to give an injection.

"The injection you just gave was saline—salt water," one of the orderlies told me. "We sometimes give them that just to make them feel better. You would be surprised at how they perk up." He laughed.

I sat by the bedsides of the soldiers at mealtimes and fed those who could not lift an implement. When I dipped my spoon to give one soldier another bite, I saw that he had died between spoonsful; the last one I gave him was drooling from his mouth.

"Don't waste the food," Ileana called to me as I rose to throw out the uneaten food. "Somebody else can finish his meal. We can't waste anything. Even the food of the dead."

A gravely wounded young soldier reached out and took my hand as I passed. He pressed my hand to his cheek, sobbing. After a moment, I stroked his head and held his face against my uniform. When I looked up, I saw that Dr. Tomescu had been watching me. He nodded curtly.

But these first days were merely the lull before the storm. The weather worsened, and winter struck with full force. Amid the freezing snows I stood outside shivering in my ragged uniform, watching in amazement as vehicle after vehicle pulled up bearing wounded. The number dwarfed what we had already been overwhelmed with. I hailed an ambulance attendant lifting out a stretcher.

"What has happened?"

"Huge battle. The Germans are being driven back. The whole army is trapped in Stalingrad. His generals want to surrender, but Hitler insists that they fight to the death. The Romanians are taking it up the rear." He paused, surveying me. "What are you? You don't look Romanian. Or maybe you do . . ."

"I am a Jew," I said.

"All this makes you happy, I suppose?" He indicated the crying, moaning men.

"Nothing makes me happy." I turned and followed the stretcher inside. Amid the chaos of wounded soldiers being dumped in the amphitheaters and hallways, I lost track of time. I forgot to eat, and Elizabeta came out to the hospital and took me back to the headquarters to feed me lunch.

"The major wants you to regain your health," she told me.

"This reminds me of the story of Hansel and Gretel," I said, nevertheless eating with good appetite.

"Oh, and am I the old witch fattening you up?" Elizabeta laughed.

"No, the major is the old witch," I said, laughing, too. "It's he that wants to consume me."

"Nevertheless," said Elizabeta, "you are surviving now. You look completely different than when those animals dragged you in. You might live through this war after all."

"I have absolutely no interest in surviving the war," I said, meaning every word.

"I once felt as you do," said Elizabeta. "But the human body is rebellious. It wants to live when our spirit wants to die. You have not seen the last of life," she said to me. "Did you ever have a . . . boyfriend? A lover?"

I looked at her and my eyes filled. "Oh, Elizabeta, I loved a young man with all my heart."

"And where is he now?"

"Probably dead. Everybody I care about is dead."

As I returned to the hospital after lunch, Ileana fell into stride with me, pushing a cart full of implements and medications.

"So . . . you are from Bessarabia," she said.

"Yes. From Yedinitz."

"Oh? They had it bad there, I hear."

"You heard right. It was the worst."

"And what did your family do in Yedinitz?"

"My mother was a dressmaker. She was—"

"Oh yes," said Ileana. "Your mother made clothes for Countess Kányádi. That is why you are so 'lucky' now." I began to protest, but I saw that she was making an ironic, biting joke and smiled a bit. "Yes. I am fortunate."

"I too was 'fortunate' with Major Dragulescu when I first came here. I was not so ugly then. He grew tired of me, and that is your good fortune."

"Oh?"

"What did you think, he only loves Jews? He has made the rounds. The only one he skipped was Lenuta. She's plenty mad about it, too." I was startled, and then I saw Ileana's mischievous smile. I relaxed a little.

"Yes, she is missing out on a lot."

"Especially his 'little woolly bear' routine," Ileana said slyly.

Before I could stop myself I was laughing. The two of us laughed together. It had been so long since I laughed that the muscles of my face and chest actually ached sharply.

"Did you sew dresses, too?"

"No," I said. "Believe it or not, I wanted to be a doctor."

"This has cured you of that, eh?" She gestured at the hospital floor.

"Not . . . exactly."

"You're not so bad after all, for a Jew. Watch yourself with the major. If he gets bored with you, he may send you to one of the camps."

"He wouldn't get the chance. Before I go to the camps, I will kill myself."

Ileana stopped. She put a hand on my wrist. "Don't."

"Why not? I'm no Catholic like you are. Do you think I fear hell? I live there now."

"But you never know what lies ahead," said Ileana.

"Yes, I do. Worse. Always worse."

"But perhaps something better. Perhaps hope."

"Ha!" I said. "Oblivion would be something better."

"Hope is what keeps me alive from day to day," said Ileana.

"Hope of what?"

Ileana shrugged. "Someday I'll tell you. Hope of something different. Maybe even peace. Maybe even love . . . someday."

"You keep your hope and I will keep . . . Major Dragulescu." We both laughed but bitterly.

Later, my medicines delivered, I walked past Ileana and Lenuta talking. I could tell somehow that they had been talking of me. They stopped, and both waved to me. I walked on, feeling for the first time, a little accepted, a tiny bit comforted.

And so, every night I endured the rutting and grunting of Major Dragulescu. He slapped and kissed me roughly, laughing and drooling; his appetite for me seemed insatiable.

"Come on! At least pretend you like it. Why do I put up with you?" He nuzzled my breasts. "Ah . . . you're filling out nicely. You were a healthy girl."

The next day, I walked up to the major's desk to deliver a sheaf of reports from Dr. Tomescu. He sat writing, as usual, while several soldiers and aides tried to look cold and indifferent, but every male eye was on me. The major looked up with his usual scowl of irritation.

"What is this?"

"The casualty reports for the week from Dr. Tomescu," I said.

The major took the papers with distaste. "I'm surprised there's room enough to list them all." He looked around. "I'm ready for a break. Good you came along."

My face remained calm, but I'm sure my eyes betrayed my desperation and humiliation. Yes, I could still feel shame. The major took my arm and walked me away, into his upstairs quarters under the stares and winks of the soldiers.

Once upstairs, he got out a bottle of liquor and poured himself a glass as I dutifully undressed.

"You might show some decorum out there," I said boldly to him.

The major laughed coarsely. "For who? Them? They'll be dead soon anyway." He drained the glass and poured himself another. "And so might you and I."

I did not respond. The major poured me a glass. "Please no," I said. "Thank you, but I'm still on duty.

Doctor Tomescu will . . ."

The major turned away and began rummaging in a drawer. "I have children, you know," he said. "Yes, even a brute like me can have a family." He pulled out a picture: a boy and a girl of about eight and ten, and a plump, nondescript woman with styled, blonde hair, posing on the beach; it looked like a Black Sea resort.

"A beautiful family," I said. After all, the war was not their fault.

Major Dragulescu stared at the picture, his face softening. "Yes, we were. A beautiful family. And happy, too, believe it or not. In a life that is now gone. My wife is dead, and my daughter . . . ran off before the war started. She's probably a whore by now." He paused reflectively staring into the past. "I was a boat builder."

"A boat builder?" I could not imagine the major as being anything but what he now was.

"I was raised in Constanta on the Black Sea. A beautiful port. My father and grandfather before him were boat builders. I married a local girl. It was a good life." He looked sharply at me, as if to summon himself back from the past.

"And you? You had a good life before this hell?"

I nodded slowly. Thinking of my family was like pressing on an open wound.

"All dead, I assume?" said the major.

"Yes. All dead."

"Where did you come from?"

"From Yedinitz. It was a beautiful town . . . once. I didn't appreciate it. I longed to go to London. Or New York."

"Didn't we all. So your family was rich, yes?"

I smiled in spite of myself. "No. Not rich in money. But in love for one another."

The major drank again and refilled his glass. "My wife, Crina, she got that . . . cancer . . . of the glands."

"Of the lymph glands?"

The major nodded. "There's a big name for it. Yes, she was cursed, the poor girl. They couldn't do anything to help her. She developed dark bruises all over her body. We brought her everywhere for treatment, even to Berlin. To the best doctors."

"I'm sorry," I said.

"I can still hear her screaming at the end. Nothing could stop the pain. The cancer was all through her body, in every organ." He paused, then hurled his glass at the wall; it exploded with the force of his grief. I flinched and ducked.

"Where . . . is your son now?"

"In the army, of course. He was a rascal, that one. Like his father." The major smiled a little and shook his head. "But I was no kind of a father after Crina died. I was never there. The neighbors had to feed my children while I went about town drunk. Starting fights."

I gently pushed my full glass in front of him, and he seized it and drank. He jerked his head at the door, which I interpreted as a signal to leave. I began to rise.

"Whaaa- . . . where are you going now?"

"I have to wash bandages tonight," I said. "It's my turn."

"Do it tomorrow. Come on back and comfort me. It's cold out there."

"If I don't clean up, we will run out of bandages tomorrow."

The major shook his head bitterly. "Go on then, get back to your blood and death. You're eager to, I can see. But I have some news for you," he said. "The Romanian government has changed its Jewish policy."

I turned my head slightly as I dressed. "Have they found a way to kill us any faster?"

"No, it's good news—for you, that is. Our accursed leader Antonescu knows the Nazis are beaten, and he's trying to chat up the Allies, like the ambitious worm he is. He'll make a separate peace if he can, but as long as the Iron Guard is murdering Jews by the thousands, Roosevelt will never deal with him. So you see? Rescue lies just ahead of you."

"All that lies ahead of me is a pile of blood and pus-soaked bandages," I replied. Major Dragulescu subsided, pouting. He thought for a moment, his stubbled chin in his palm.

"And something else, I don't know if I should even tell you. You may decide to leave me." He watched for a response, but I gave none. I had discovered that with such a mercurial captor, the less I shared about myself, the safer I was. He was capable of misinterpreting everything I said.

"It appears that Antonescu is letting some Jews from Transnistria emigrate to Palestine. You see, he's throwing a sop to the world Jewish conspiracy."

I turned my head. "You mean to Auschwitz, not Palestine, don't you? More Nazi trickery."

"Ah . . . you're no fun at all," said the major. "Every piece of good news I give you, you look for the worms in it." He reached out and put his hand under my skirt. "Show some kindness toward your little woolly bear." He grabbed me roughly by the hair and bent my neck backward. "Or he will rip your pretty face off." I smelled the liquor on his breath and knew that he was capable of doing what he said. Later, when it was too late, he would be deeply remorseful.

I closed my eyes for a moment. When I opened them, I made sure to smile teasingly at him. I reached out and began to fondle his body. "I thought you like when women play hard to get," I said to him.

The major's face softened and distorted with lust. "So that's your game. Yes, tease me some more. That's the little Jewgirl I like."

I climbed atop the major in my nurses' uniform as he writhed with pleasure. But I was far away in my mind from the disgusting charade that my body was participating in; I was in Palestine with Mihail. We were walking through an orange grove, free and proud, together in each others' arms. And people were greeting us: Papa, Mama, and little Jacob, who danced around us playing his violin. I chose the piece carefully—a Bach prelude, as lovely as the blue sky and the shiny green leaves and the luscious fruit so brilliant and fresh for the picking.

Later, I hurried through the encampment toward the hospital. Two officers were talking as I passed and cold as it was, I slowed to listen.

"The Russian front is kaput," a tall officer was saying to a shorter man with his arm in a sling. "For my money, the war is over."

"Yes," said the shorter man, "the war is lost, but the killing will go on for years."

"Don't be so sure," replied the tall officer. "Antonescu is a fool, but not an idiot. My money, the war will be over by the new year."

"It's a bet!"

"May we both live to collect." The two officers fumbled in their pockets as I walked on, wondering if I dared to hope for an end to the war.

Still lost in thought, I entered the chilly, moan-filled hospital. Despite the fire roaring in a large fireplace at one end, the air was so cold you could see your breath. The wounded soldiers huddled shivering under their blankets.

I entered the supply area and hauled out huge sacks of bloody bandages. Nearby, I found the wheeled canvas carry-all and loaded the sacks into it. As I was tugging the carry-all toward the laundry area, my eye fell on some medical instruments set out for a surgery, including a scalpel.

Suddenly, I halted and eyed the scalpel; looking around I saw that nobody was paying any particular attention to me. I picked up the scalpel and looked at my wrists; slowly, I traced the instrument across the blue veins. I closed my eyes.

In one moment I could end my misery and terror forever. One deep slash. But I almost laughed—what stayed my hand? You may not believe this, but I feared infection! How could a corpse become infected? Nevertheless, I slowly replaced the scalpel, speaking to it *sotto voce*: "Just wait for me, my friend," I told the gleaming silver knife. "Stay sharp. I will be back for you one of these days. Do not forget me, and I will not forget you, either."

As I turned away, I heard groaning and crying from a stretcher crowding past me and my odious load of bandages. Looking down, I saw to my shock the very

Romanian soldier who had killed my mother and Jacob. I could not believe my eyes. I knew his fat red face and thick lips as if they had been burned onto my eyes.

In my mind, I instantly flashed back to the Yedinitz ghetto where we had huddled on that last ghastly day. All around us was a wasteland of makeshift tents and lean-tos with weak, traumatized people lying about in the dust.

In my fevered memory, I once again saw Mama falling backward coughing blood. I saw Jacob lying in the dust writhing and gasping. Dying Priva raised herself on her arms, crying out.

I nearly reeled with shock as I gazed upon the face of the monster. His tormented eyes gazed back at me without any recognition whatsoever. He did not remember me. His collarbone had been shot away; it was bandaged with a filthy, bloody rag; his uniform was covered with blood. Nevertheless, I saw that his wound was survivable.

"Hey, nursing sister," called out the attendant who was transporting him, "get your cart out of my way. This fellow is badly hurt." Dazed, I followed his gurney with my eyes as I mechanically moved the cart aside and continued down the hallway with it.

The thought suddenly came to me that it was God who had put him in this hospital, in my very hands. I returned to the table and snatched up the scalpel again and put it into my pocket, then moved my cart resolutely after the gurney with the murderer writhing and moaning atop it.

A part of my duties was to collect the bloody bandages that the nurses had thrown into baskets, take them into a vast laundry room, and wash them by hand. I pushed my loaded carry-all to a washing station and dipped water from a steaming cauldron into a tub-sized basin. Around me, other nurses and orderlies were laundering blankets, bandages, and sheets by hand.

I mixed ashes from a barrel with lye and other chemicals to concoct a harsh, primitive detergent. Then I began to launder the bandages. As the water turned bloody, I dumped it into a massive drain in the floor and refilled my basin. My hands grew rough and chapped from the chemicals and the hot water, but the others had assured me that they would toughen up, and indeed, after a while it didn't bother me at all.

As I worked today, I would stop occasionally and touch my pocket with the scalpel in it. When I was finished washing the bandages and the rinse water ran clear, I would wring out the bandages and hang them on a line near the large fire to dry.

But now, just as I was finishing my chore and hanging the last of the bandages, Ileana came up behind me.

"Little one," she said, "I need you to take my overnight shift tonight." Ileana and I had developed the beginnings of a friendship. When she saw that I worked hard and treated the wounded men kindly, she and the others had begun to accept me. After all, I had heard them saying, "she"—meaning me—didn't choose to be a Jew.

I turned in surprise now, and Ileana took my damp hand in both of hers, smiling with a teasing expression.

"I have a . . . rendezvous tonight with one of the soldiers. He leaves in the morning. So we are going to have a little tryst to send him off and give him something to remember me by."

"Of course I'd help you out," I told her, "but the major is expecting me."

"You're okay," Ileana said. "There's a Nazi big shot arriving tonight from the Russian front. In fact, two of them. German generals or something. The major will be entertaining him late into the night."

Relief flooded through me at this unexpected reprieve. "Of course. I'll work your shift," I told Ileana.

"Now listen, little rabbit," she said and stroked my hair, "there's one more thing. I told my man that I would do his wash for him. But if his buddies find out, we'll have no peace, they'll all want their filthy drawers laundered by hand, and we have enough to do to just keep up with the patients." I smiled. "So he is leaving his bundle outside his barracks D-4 near the woods," Ileana said. "You go pick it up for us, all right?"

I nodded, and Ileana hugged me joyously. "Who is your boyfriend?" I asked her, because usually Ileana was dour and rarely expressed any excitement and pleasure. Not that there was any reason to, of course, the way we lived among the dead and dying.

"His name is Antonin," Ileana said with a twinkle. She busied herself measuring out medications while she talked to me. "So . . . have you ever been in love?"

"To the depth and height of my soul," I said. I smiled at the very thought of Mihail; just the pleasure of speaking about him lit up my features.

Ileana looked deeply into my eyes. "Yes, I can see you have known love." My eyes filled with tears even as I smiled at the memories that came flooding. "You believe him to be dead?" Ileana asked.

"Everybody I love is dead," I replied. "I don't dare think of him with any hope. I live only in the past, in my memories, and I'm grateful for those."

Ileana gave me a searching look, she took my arms and squeezed them, and then turned and flew from the room.

I continued rinsing my basin, mingling my tears with the water as I emptied it out. I could not easily stop the tears from flowing, so I ignored them and went on about my duties.

I found out later from Elizabeta about the Nazi bigwigs who soon arrived: As the sun was setting, a polished Mercedes Benz pulled up to the headquarters. The Romanian officers had already assembled to greet and salute the big shot occupants as they emerged from the car with all their self-important airs.

The occupants were the veteran Nazi Manfred von Killinger and SS officer Gustav Richter. Major Dragulescu emerged from his headquarters to bow, salute, and heartily shake hands. Trays with glasses of fine brandy were brought out to them and presented before they even came indoors.

From a window facing the courtyard, I watched the Nazis greet Major Dragulescu. I could feel my eyes narrow and my lip curl in involuntary disgust.

The library had once been beautiful and elegant but had suffered great degradation and casual destruction. Nevertheless, I had seen that the Romanians had made an effort to rehabilitate it and neatened it up, polishing the tables that hadn't yet been used as firewood and dusting off and arranging the remaining books.

The visiting Nazis relaxed with Major Dragulescu before the cheerful fire. With candles lit, the ambience was almost cozy and civilized, giving the lie to the bloody reality of the horrors and deaths taking place all around us.

Romanian officers, all dressed up and boots polished for the occasion, now gathered in small convivial groups, chatting, complimenting the Nazis with small talk. When the fire died down a little, some of them grabbed a few books and threw them into the flames.

Peeking in at Elizabeta's side, I saw the Nazis scowl at this wanton destruction. They considered themselves cultured and civilized, I noted, superior to the Romanians. I saw the contempt they could barely hide when they observed the Iron Guard. Aides brought in platters of dried fruit and cheese that Elizabeta and I had prepared in the kitchen. The Nazis and Iron Guard officers nibbled at the platters.

"They'll leave plenty over," Elizabeta told me. Her plump cheeks were flushed with anticipation. In honor of the Nazis' arrival the major had broken out a hoard of dainties and delicacies.

"So. Standartenfuhrer Killinger," the major said, "explain to me why you remain confident that Germany will win the war."

Killinger looked keenly at the major. "I won't insult your intelligence with hopeful fabrications, Major. Stalingrad has been . . . a setback. But the German people have vast resources in reserve, plus super-weapons in development that will more than even up the score."

"Ahhh, 'secret super-weapons' now! A Hollywood movie! Forgive a country bumpkin like myself, but why didn't you unleash some of those weapons on the Russians before they destroyed your Sixth Army?"

Killinger bridled. "There's a lot you don't know, Major. But your excellent brandy perhaps convinces you that you do and loosens your tongue."

"In other words, you are telling me to shut up," said Major Dragulescu amiably, "and I defer. I admit my ignorance is vast."

The major raised his glass. "To heroes fallen and victories to come." The Nazis, appeased, also raised their glasses and they all drank their toast.

"And where does all of this turmoil leave Romania?" the major pressed on, and I almost winced at his nerve in again confronting the Nazi.

"Where she has always stood, Major. As a valued ally and trusted friend. I hope your Herr Antonescu doesn't let himself be cowed or stampeded by this transient setback...."

The major started to speak, but Killinger raised his voice to speak over him. "... into losing faith and making a separate peace with the Allies. It would be the worst possible thing for Romania."

Gustav Richter, the other Nazi, broke in: "... particularly when your country is nearly *Judenrein*. Cleansed of your Jewish infestation."

Major Dragulescu said, with an edge to his voice, "Yes ... you've been quite efficient at that, at least."

Richter replied, also with an edge to his voice. "And your own Iron Guard have been, shall we say, even ahead of the game? Very effective at purging the Jew from your midst. We almost couldn't have done it better." And he gave a little laugh.

"With all respect," said the major, "there are other issues in this war besides the Jews."

"Now that's where you're wrong," said Richter. "Don't you see, Major? The Jew is what this war has always been about." Major Dragulescu did not answer.

"The Jews and their American banker friends were not satisfied with wrecking Europe's entire economic infrastructure in the Great War. It wasn't enough that their greed plunged the world into the worst Depression in history, causing millions to starve while they lined their pockets."

"And how is that the fault of Jewish cobblers and . . . schoolteachers?" The major was unable to hold himself back any longer.

"Ho, Major!" Richter replied while Killinger strolled over to the library and studied the books. "You are yourself in need of a teacher. An education! Jews are parasites, all of them, throughout history."

Major Dragulescu started to speak but instead gulped down the rest of his drink and immediately poured himself another glass. He sat down and watched the fire.

But Richter was on a rant. "And now their leaders start yet another war, so that they can profiteer from arming America to slaughter the German—and the Romanian—people. Forcing Britain to fight her German cousins when both countries wanted only peace. . . . There's no end to their evil manipulations."

Richter continued to grow more excited. "The Jew has simply got to be eliminated, Major, and if the German nation does nothing else, we will have accomplished that! The extirpation of that foul race." He pounded his fist on a nearby table. "Down. To. The. Very. Seed."

Major Dragulescu shifted uncomfortably on his chair. He caught the eye of Killinger, who looked away quickly. Meanwhile, Richter strutted, enjoying his own ranting rhetoric.

". . . or like the choking weeds they are, the Jews will

spring back up and continue along their path toward world domination. Just as if all our sacrifices had never happened. As if our martyrs had not given their heart's blood, the sainted mothers their only sons. My God, Major, your hospital is filled with the flower of German, *and* Romanian youth. And why?"

"Yes," said the major. "Why?"

"The Jew, Major. The cursed Jew."

Killinger, looking bored, continued to peruse the remaining books in the shelves. He removed a couple, opened and read them.

"Major, you have some excellent first editions here. English authors. And a few Americans. With your permission, before you burn them all, I would like to go through and bring a few of them back with me to Berlin."

"Be my guest, of course," said Major Dragulescu. "I myself do not read English, as you know."

Back at the hospital after my dinner break, I bustled about tucking in patients, giving shots and medications, adjusting catheters, and so forth. I paused by the bed of the now delirious Iron Guard soldier who had murdered my mother and read his chart hanging at the foot of the bed. A nearby soldier looked up.

"He needs pain medicine, nurse. He is very bad. He does not want to bother you."

I nodded, walked over to the nurses' station, and went through the medications. I removed a couple of pills from a bottle and returned with a glass of water. The soldier roused and sat up on one elbow to take his medication gratefully.

"Thank you. You are an angel." I did not reply but moved away. I was trying to think of a way that I could kill him without arousing suspicion. I was so busy thinking that I almost forgot about the favor I had promised Ileana.

I glanced at the clock, then paused by a coatrack and put on a light coat. I moved toward the door and stopped at the desk of the supervising nurse, an older woman.

"Excuse me, I . . . have a small errand I must run," I told her.

She looked up with an expression of disbelief. "At this time of night? You'll get yourself killed out there!"

"No, really," I said, "it's something I promised, a favor for a friend. I'll only be gone a few minutes." I put my hand on the door.

The nurse shrugged. "Don't try to escape," she said, scrutinizing me. "There's no place to go. Watch yourself, and don't get shot."

"I'll be back before you know it," I told her.

"What kind of a friend asks that sort of favor?" she muttered.

I wrapped myself in the warmest blanket I could find and let myself out of the hospital door into the harsh air. In the shadow of the building, I was immediately shrouded in darkness. Although it was getting toward spring, the weather was still wintry. Often we found our water supplies frozen in the morning. Only in the height of daytime could you begin to feel winter beginning to release its grip.

I walked quickly through the headquarters courtyard toward the military encampment. I could hear the soldiers talking and laughing coarsely among themselves; I could only pray that they would ask me to identify myself before shooting. Many of them knew who I was now, since I had taken care of them or their comrades. Their fear of the major kept their lustful impulses in check, although I had known some of them before I met the major and bore the bruises and scars to attest to it.

Looking toward the headquarters courtyard, I could see the lights blazing in the windows of the main rooms where Major Dragulescu was entertaining the visiting Nazis. I allowed my feet to crunch loudly on the frozen ground and cleared my throat. It was safer to make noise and announce my presence.

"Halt!" came the command at last. "Who goes?"

"It's Daniela from the hospital," I answered loudly. "The nurse."

"You? What are you doing out here at night?"

I tried to make my tremulous voice sound shyly flirtatious. "I'm on an errand for a friend. A favor."

"Ahhh. A boyfriend then? The major will hear of this."

"No, naughty boy, it's not a favor for myself."

"Not getting enough manly action from the major? That old fart. Come here, you minx, and do us a quick favor. We won't tell."

I edged away, half expecting a bullet in the back or to be grabbed and dragged off. They were capable of raping me and threatening death to me if I told.

"Don't get lost, Jew. You should have brought a torch."

"I know where I have to go."

The soldiers snickered and laughed among themselves. I continued making my way toward the barracks, which were closer to the forest.

As I walked, a hand suddenly covered my mouth, and I was dragged off struggling into a small copse of woods.

"Daniela. Don't scream. It's I, Mihail. Stop struggling.

Don't make a sound."

I couldn't stop myself from gasping. In the near blackness I strained my eyes, trying to make out his form. I reached up and felt the side of his face. My knees buckled, but he caught me.

"I'm here with the partisans," he spoke in a harsh whisper. "We're here to kill Richter and Killinger."

My mouth fell open in shock. For a moment I was too dumbfounded to speak. We scanned one another's faces greedily. "Mihail," I finally whispered. "Do not touch me. I . . . I am defiled."

"You don't have to say anything," Mihail whispered, holding his cheek to mine. The intensity of his words almost burned my skin. I suddenly clung to him desperately.

"My Daniela," he said, "more has happened to me than I can tell. We are both different, but our love is unchanged. Tonight, though, there is just one thing in the world that matters. We have to kill Richter. He is working with Eichmann to deport thousands of Romanian Jews to Auschwitz before Antonescu makes peace with the Allies, which could happen any day. He must die now."

"How can I help?"

"We need a way into headquarters. You have to let us in when you go to the major."

I turned my head away in shame. "You know then what I have become. Mihail, I am corrupt. I am a dead person."

"Hush," he said, stroking my face, "you are my Rose of Sharon."

The hot tears coursed down my cheeks, and we embraced as if we had only a few moments to live, as I then believed we did. He kissed me passionately as ever—more than ever. We both knew death and untold suffering now, which made our kisses sweeter than they had ever been.

But Mihail pulled away again. "We have a job to do. There will be time for us later, God willing."

My mouth fell open at this passionate atheist's mention of God.

"You have changed," I said. I took his hands and kissed their palms. I sank to my knees. "Whatever you ask of me I will, if I die doing it."

"Ileana is one of us," Mihail said. "She sent you out here. You must never give her away even by the slightest sign or word. You now hold her life in your hands."

"I understand."

"Daniela, are you ready?"

I nodded. "You know I am." I spoke quickly. "I use a servant's entrance when I come back from hospital duty. I will bring your people in that way."

"Do you know where Richter and Killinger are sleeping?"

"I think so. The aides were preparing their rooms this morning."

"Here." He thrust a package into my hands. "This is the dirty laundry you were sent to collect. Go back now."

I clasped Mihail desperately and we kissed again.

"Someday," Mihail whispered into my ear.

"Someday," I replied.

He slipped away from me without a sound and disappeared into the darkness. I collected myself and moments later emerged from the bushes holding the satchel of laundry. By now the moon had come out, illuminating the grounds. A few moments longer and we would have stood out in the bright rays. Now I hurriedly returned along the path, my feet once again disturbing the gravel on the frozen ground.

I stopped and called out to the sentries. "It is only I again, fellows."

"Did you give as good as you got, baby?"

"I did what I was told to do. My . . . duties." The sentries laughed crudely, making dirty jokes and double entendres in their dialect.

"You can't fool us. You cannot get enough of your 'duties.' You should come visit us more often. We will show you what real men have."

"No . . . I cannot," I said, as if I were tempted. "I am loyal to the major." This provoked peals of laughter and more jokes.

"What are you carrying? Let me see!" The guard took the packet and opened it.

"Phew! She does his laundry, too! I want some of this pampering!" All of them roared with laughter now.

"Come back by when you're off, little minx."

"I just might," I said as I slipped away with my packet.

"Let me get my hands on you, you won't soon forget me." I almost shuddered with revulsion but managed to laugh, low and slyly.

"Take out your lust on the major. He's been in a better mood since he has you warming his bed."

They laughed again as I neared the hospital, their obscene cries escorting me up to the very door. The moment I tugged it open, their laughter was instantly replaced by the usual moans and cries of agony, shouts for water, and prayers to God and Jesus to help them.

The supervising nurse glanced up as I entered,

breathing hard, more with stunned shock than with exertion. "You got a touch of frostbite," she said looking at my flushed cheeks. "Go put some salve on your cheeks. The major can't abide rough skin. You will be tossed out!" She laughed at her own joke, and once again I had to fake my convivial laughter.

"I'm fine, really," I said.

"What do you have there? No, don't tell me. I can smell it from here. And no more sneaking around the grounds like this at night. Your patients need you."

"Yes, Ma'am," I said.

"You watch yourself. You know which side your bread is buttered on."

"Yes, Ma'am."

As I threaded my way among the beds, I saw the Iron Guard murderer of my mother and brother sleeping peacefully at last. He looked improved. I seated myself on a wooden chair nearby to wait for Ileana and began to roll bandages, but my hands shook so violently that I could barely control them.

Ileana appeared at last. "Did you get what you went for?" she asked me, picking up the package at my feet.

"Yes. I . . . I . . ." But Ileana made a quick warning motion to say no more. "When are you off duty?" she asked.

"An hour. more or less."

Ileana busied herself rolling bandages along with me.

"You know what you have to do?" she whispered. I nodded, and Ileana whispered curtly, "Many thousands of our people are relying on you now. On us." I nodded and began rolling bandages again, now with much steadier hands.

At last I glanced at the clock, which read 2:30 A.M. I

stretched and rose to go off duty. I wended my way among my charges one last time. But as I made my last check of the soldiers, I suddenly noticed that one of them, a liver injury, had grown considerably worse.

I bent over his bed and saw blood on his stomach bandages. His wound was bleeding out. I ran for help.

"What is it now?" asked the supervising nurse, opening her reddened eyes.

"The patient, Hans, with the shrapnel in his liver. He is hemorrhaging."

"I knew he would take a turn. I'll get Doctor Tomescu. Watch my desk."

She rose and hurried away. I looked at her desk and noticed a romance novel hidden away among the folders and charts. So the old terror had a love life, even if only in her mind.

I signaled a nurse to take my place at her desk and returned to my patient's bed. By now blood was dripping onto the floor. Other soldiers had awakened at his moans.

"Help me!" Hans cried out, terrified.

As the other patients watched, I tried helplessly to staunch the flow. Desperately I checked the clock as Dr. Tomescu and the supervising nurse came running.

Dr. Tomescu leaned over the patient. "Well, Hans," he said, "it seems you need surgery yet again. You are keeping us busy tonight." The doctor spoke to me tersely. "No time for the operating room. We'll do it here. Go get the plasma."

The supervising nurse grabbed a partition on wheels and pushed it into place to shield the bed. She ran off and returned with a cone of ether and held it over Hans' face. Meanwhile I set up an IV with the plasma bottle hanging to replace his fluids.

Another nurse wheeled up a cart of instruments. Dr. Tomescu exposed the boy's stomach, swabbed hurriedly with iodine, then took a scalpel and cut down into the abdomen as I stood by to assist. The clock now read 2:36 A.M. Moments passed as Dr. Tomescu tried to repair the hemorrhaging liver.

"More plasma," he ordered, and I moved quickly to switch out the bottle. "I'm losing him. Is there a pulse?"

I hurriedly started the plasma and then reached out to check the boy's wrist.

Dr. Tomescu shouted, "Well? Speak up! Am I operating on a corpse? Does he have a pulse?"

I felt desperately for a beat. Then I closed my eyes and nodded. "Very fast, thready and irregular." The clock ticked on.

"How is he now?"

"Yes," I said, "his pulse is growing stronger."

Dr. Tomescu beamed. "I think we caught it. You did right to check him one last time. He could have bled out. Look, his color is coming up even as we speak. These farm boys are impossible to kill. Come on, Hans. Live. Live!"

The clock now read 3:00 A.M.

"I'm closing. The hemorrhage has stopped. Now only time will tell. Daniela, you stay with him tonight."

My heart sank. "But the major—"

"Dammit. To hell with the major. This boy needs a nurse by his side. I'll answer to the major."

I stood speechless. Dr. Tomescu thought for a moment. "On the other hand, you really don't have the training.... Go get the supervising nurse. He needs a steadier hand than yours. Not that I am not grateful to you for sounding the alarm. You did very well at the surgery." The supervising nurse came running up. "You stay with him," Dr. Tomescu told her. "Let the major have his little diversion." He gave a snort of contempt. The nurse nodded but cast a suspicious look at me that froze my blood.

I took to my heels and fled the hospital at a dead run for the major's quarters, hoping I was not too late. I crossed the compound and waved to the sentry guarding the headquarters.

"Hallo!" I shouted. "Who is on duty tonight?"

"It's me, your best boyfriend Tadeo," came a voice.

"Hello, Tadeo," I called out. He was a friendly fellow who was one of Elizabeta's favorites. She would often sneak him tidbits.

"You're late getting off," he said.

"We had a hemorrhage all of a sudden. A liver injury. But I think Dr. Tomescu has saved him. It was touch and go."

"Dr. Tomescu is a miracle worker."

"I am exhausted."

"Sleep well ... If he lets you."

"Hush, you!" I laughed along with him.

I walked around to the servants' entrance at the side of the building. As soon as I arrived, Mihail appeared beside me. Two other partisans, armed and clad in black, were standing with him. Quietly, I opened the door and checked the empty hallway.

Elizabeta instantly appeared at the top of the stairs leading to the offices and living quarters.

"Daniela, you're late!"

"Dr. Tomescu had to do emergency surgery right in

the ward. There wasn't even time to take the patient to the operating room. He was hemorrhaging so badly."

"Oh my God. Did he die?"

"No, I think he is improved."

"I don't know how you do it," said Elizabeta. "If I see a single drop of blood I grow faint, old as I am. Come have a little snack with me, darling. The guests left over so much food. If we don't eat it, the soldiers will take it all tomorrow. I've made you tea."

"Oh, Elizabeta, I am all in," I cried out. "I cannot even drag my feet upstairs. I hope the major is asleep."

"Go ahead and hope, for all the good it'll do you. He's a night owl, that one. Well, I'll put away a little bit for your breakfast tomorrow. But don't be too surprised if it's gone."

"Go ahead and help yourself."

"They had stuffed eggs, gorgonzola cheese, oh I can't even name all the dainties! Potatoes with sour cream. I licked their plates, I can tell you."

"Good night, Elizabeta. Have as much as you want."

The moment she went away, the partisans glided in and stole through the semi-dark hallways of the old house. I guided them upstairs using a different route, a hallway that didn't pass the kitchen.

We arrived in the library, which still smelled of the cigars, brandy, and food. Half-filled glasses sat on the polished cherrywood tables. Hugging the walls, we passed through the library; I could see the partisans' tense faces under their dark camouflage; their eyes shone in the dying glow of the fire's embers. I tried not to stare at Mihail, but I could feel his presence within and around me.

After what seemed an eternity, we arrived at the

staircase leading up to the living quarters. We had to ascend completely exposed. Had anyone come into the room they would have seen all four of us—Mihail, me, and the two partisans—hugging their rifles.

I checked the upstairs hallway and signaled the men. We passed along it quietly, barely breathing.

Slowly, I opened the door of one of the rooms. In the bed, Manfred Killinger lay on his back snoring. I ducked out and pointed inside the room.

"Killinger," I said in a soft whisper. Mihail nodded and signaled silently to a partisan, who noiselessly entered the room with a garotte. The man was stocky, and his arms and shoulders bulged with muscle. Quickly and smoothly, he slipped the garotte around Killinger's neck and yanked it tight. His breath had been completely choked off before Killinger even awoke. As he roused and struggled, Mihail and the other partisan held his arms and legs to prevent him from thrashing and perhaps kicking over a table or a lamp. I watched in horror as the life passed from the man's body and he succumbed. It took only four minutes to extinguish all life, turning him from a sentient human being into a livid corpse.

Quickly, the partisan removed and coiled the garrote and motioned to me to move on. We closed Killinger's door and walked a few more paces down the hallway. In the silence, we heard footsteps coming up the stairs and a male voice humming a soldier's tune. Mihail and the partisans quickly returned to Killinger's room and closed the door behind them.

Major Dragulescu appeared at the head of the stairs and spotted me; he broke into a grin. "What are you prowling around for, kitten?" he said boisterously, still drunk. "Why aren't you in bed? And you're out of breath. Are you panting for love?"

"I . . . just got back. We . . . had an emergency at the hospital. Dr. Tomescu had to operate. I ran all the way back as soon as I could."

Major Dragulescu stood at his door. "Well, I had quite a night listening to those two Nazi bores. You'd think they had single-handedly won the war. The truth is, they're on the ropes, all of them. Hitler's house of cards is crumbling." The major came close and slapped my rear. "Now get in and get to it. I need some comforting tonight. Whew. I'll be glad to see the last of their arrogant Prussian asses, that couple of egotistical dolts."

"I'll be right there," I said. The major stopped.

"What now?"

"I need to . . . wash myself. The operation was very bloody."

"And I'm squeamish about blood?" He pinched my cheek. "Dainty little mouse. You're teasing me. I should throw you down on the floor and have you right here."

"Then you would spoil all the fun," I replied, trying to sound playful.

"All right, all right. Do your 'toilette.' But hurry up. And you had better look good for me after all this delay."

He turned around, opened his bedroom door, and slammed it shut behind him.

I returned to Killinger's room and beckoned to Mihail and the partisans. We continued down the hallway. I opened another door—the room was empty. We had nearly reached the end of the hallway and the major's bedroom.

I opened the last door very quietly and looked in.

Richter was sitting on his bed, masturbating to a photo of a provocatively posed naked young man in heavy make-up and silk stockings. He startled at the sight of me and tried to conceal the picture, but there was no hiding it. I held my finger to my lips provocatively, as if I had come for sex. Because he was caught in a compromising act, Richter whispered. "And who the hell are you?"

Seeming disappointed, I replied, "I am here for your pleasure, Mein Herr." This caused Richter to pause long enough for Mihail to jump in with his gun. Richter grabbed for a knife on the bedstand, but before he reached it, Mihail fired a burst of bullets into his chest from the doorway.

Instantly, the major emerged from his room with his revolver blazing, but Mihail quickly wheeled and shot him, too.

We stood silently for a moment as the bloody corpses slumped amid the smoke of the gunfire. From downstairs I heard Elizabeta screaming for me to hide. I motioned to the partisans not to shoot her.

There was nowhere to go as Elizabeta opened the front door and screamed out into the darkness for help. We could hear her shouting that we were under attack as soldiers entered the living room downstairs. The partisans quickly smashed a window in Richter's room with their guns and disappeared out into the foliage below. Mihail beckoned me.

"Jump!" Still wearing my restrictive nurse's uniform, I climbed through the window and leaped outward toward a young juniper tree beneath. I broke some branches, landing scratched but unhurt, and Mihail landed almost on top of me.

Hearing shots, I ran with the partisans toward the woods at the back of the house. We disappeared into a thick copse of evergreens that bordered on the soldiers' encampment; I could see them running out toward the house.

But suddenly bullets started hitting the trees around us. "They're just firing into the woods," Mihail hissed to me. "They don't know we're here." Just then I saw him stumble. I thought he had tripped on a root and paused to help him up, but I saw that he had been hit by a random bullet in the dark.

My trained nurse's eye realized at once that the wound was fatal. He waved me on, coughed blood, and began to strangle, his eyes wild. Behind me, a partisan materialized and quickly shot Mihail in the head. He grabbed me by the arm and yanked me away.

"He's gone. Run!" he shouted. "Follow us." My legs barely holding me, I stumbled along behind the partisan, who kept looking back and urging me to go faster. Now bullets began landing all around us, but I realized that they were only firing wildly; they did not know where to aim as we dodged and wove among the trees and branches on the ground. Mihail had certainly been hit by a random shot and not by aim. I kept thinking of his face at the end, his eyes desperately seeking mine. Why had I not embraced him? It had all happened so fast it seemed like a dream.

We fled deeper into the woods, and now searchlights began to shine around us, illuminating the trees. Bullets kept hitting the tree trunks, gouging out chunks of wood that flew in all directions.

Behind us sirens began going off. I ran grimly and

mechanically now, my shoes pounding the dirt. Another partisan was hit in the leg, and I leaped to help him without pausing; we dragged him with us as he grunted and panted trying to run on the injured leg.

"It's a flesh wound," said one of the partisans to the injured man. "It missed the bone."

"*Dayenu,*" enough, said the man between his teeth. The blood was pouring down his calf from a deep hole; I used the scalpel in my pocket to cut off the tie that held the apron of my uniform. Pausing for a moment to grab a stick from the ground I fashioned a crude tourniquet on the run. Then we dragged the man along, limping on his wounded leg.

I could see that the partisans knew where they were going; they had preemptively mapped out an escape route. We arrived at a shallow river, crossed easily, and ran through the muddy furrows of a newly plowed field. Gradually, the firing and shouts faded away in another direction.

"There we are," panted the partisan who had been shot in the leg. "Thank God!" He pointed to a small truck parked at the end of the field with two men sitting in it, smoking. At the sight of us they jumped into action and helped haul the wounded man into the truck bed. We jumped in after him, and the truck roared away. We covered ourselves under thick canvas in the back. We slewed wildly at first on the wet road, then gained momentum and sped east toward the rising sun.

Under the tarpaulin, I lay on my stomach panting, numb with shock. Now the full realization that Mihail was dead flooded through me; rage, anguish, and confusion battered my aching head, overwhelming me. I had

had him and then lost him cruelly before my very eyes without the span of a few hours. I wished that I could go mad and develop amnesia and forget all I had ever known.

I realized, too, that I would probably never see Philippa again; any chance of getting away from the war to a safer place was no longer possible. My fate and whatever future I was destined to have now lay with the partisans. With the major dead and my collaboration exposed, my life was worth nothing; my term as a prisoner and a concubine was over. But I had escaped the Romanians forever. We finally dared to peek from under the canvas and emerged to clutch at the slatted wooden sides of the truck as it fled and jounced down the rutted road.

"Mihail, Mihail!" I buried my head in my arms and sobbed. The partisan beside me watched for a moment, his face contorted with cynicism and scorn. I was sure he thought of me as no more than an Iron Guard whore. And that was what I was. Why was I even alive in my dishonored state? Yes, I had suffered, but so had everybody else. Perhaps he thought an honorable death was superior to my warming the bed of an Iron Guard officer and eating dainties from his table. Nursing enemy soldiers and saving their lives to recover and go fight again, killing Allied troops and Jews.

"What are you crying for?" the partisan finally blurted. I realized he was making a rough effort to comfort me. "Mihail died fast and well. You should be proud. Celebrate him! He succeeded in our mission and died knowing that Killinger and Richter were dead. It was a perfect end."

I did not reply. He had turned his face away to hide

his own tears. I gave way again to violent sobs as the truck jolted. Another partisan finally offered me a cigarette, and I took it, my hands shaking.

"*Genug,* enough. Leave off the tears already," he said. "Save your strength for avenging him by killing Nazi and Iron Guard swine." He and I smoked, watching the sun emerge above the horizon.

Soon the truck began to roll more smoothly. Over the roar of the engine, somebody in the cab was chanting a Jewish prayer for the dead. I dozed and suddenly jerked awake. A partisan was sleeping against my shoulder.

The truck stopped briefly, and the wounded partisan was placed in the cab. The man who had been riding next to the driver came into the back of the truck, and we took off again.

"You're Daniela," he said to me. "I'm Schmuel."

"That's my father's name," I blurted.

"Is your father dead?"

"Of course. Where are we going?"

"Over the Russian border. They won't follow us there, the lickspittle cowards. The Romanians don't have the stomach for this war anymore. And the Nazis are in retreat back to their own stinking country. The Russians are driving them west like a herd of cattle now. They think they will make a final stand on the borders of Germany. But it won't do them any good."

"So Germany has lost the war?"

"What do you think? The Americans invaded Europe. They're fighting their way through Italy now."

"They never told us this."

"No," said the partisan, "they wouldn't, would they? Have to keep up 'morale.'" He laughed bitterly. "Romania can't surrender fast enough. They're licking Roosevelt's boots and pleading for a separate peace. That means we may be able to bring some of the remaining Jews out and get them to Palestine."

"Oh my God," I said. "Are there still Jews even alive?"

"Not many," the partisan said. "But our people will survive now. We will build a Jewish homeland. Perhaps you will be a part of that."

"And Mihail didn't live to see it," I said.

"He loved you very much, you should know."

"He did?" I said, recalling for a moment the schoolgirl again that I had been a lifetime ago. I was hungry to hear more about Mihail, to speak his name.

"He couldn't stop talking about you," said Schmuel. "He planned to marry you. The thought of you sustained him."

"I loved him every waking moment," I said.

"Then you will do his memory justice in your life, I know," Schmuel told me. "It's time to face the future. There is much work still to be done." His eyes narrowed and glittered. "Many missions still to carry out. We are deployed with the Russian partisans, helping them destroy the German supply lines. We are starving the bastards as they flee. The Luftwaffe is kaput. We don't even worry about being attacked from the air anymore. Meanwhile the Allies are bombing the hell out of Germany. They're carpeting the cities with incendiary bombs. Turning Germany into a torch."

I said, "They are fire-bombing civilians?"

"What do the Germans expect? The British and Americans didn't start the war. But they will finish it. Sometimes the napalm they drop is so intense it turns into tornadoes of fire. Whole cities go up in flames. That is Hitler's gift to his people. And still they fight on."

"My God."

"So you believe in God after all of this."

"Of course not," I said. "It's just a turn of phrase I use."

"I, too," Schmuel said. We laughed. He leaned forward and bellowed to the truck's driver. "We got the bastards. And a Romanian general to boot!"

The driver pumped his fist in the air from the window.

"He was ... only a major," I said. For some bizarre reason, I felt bad that the major had died. I should have celebrated the death of my enslaver. But our relationship had not been so simple.

"Major. General. Whatever. We shot the pig." He leaned back and sprawled against the side of the truck, looking at me keenly. "What? You liked him after all that?"

"I could have killed him myself," I said. "But being a slave corrupts and warps a person. I am as defiled as a woman can be."

"You don't have to apologize for anything," said Schmuel. "Whatever you did is in the past. You did it to survive. You are a Jewish daughter. Nothing can change that. The Jews need people like you to build the homeland. Young and strong and skilled. And you're where you belong now. If you allow guilt to invade your mind you will go mad."

"I am mad anyway," I said. "I always thought I was crazy as a child."

"No," Schmuel said, "what's crazy is Naziism. What's crazy is killing people who never harmed you. The Germans killed their own as well as the Jews. They even killed German Christian children born with a limp.

That's madness."

"I'm Jonah," said the other partisan, who had been listening to Schmuel and me talking. "So you were a nurse? Did they know you're a Jew?"

I nodded and suddenly thought of Ileana.

"What about Ileana?" I said to Schmuel in a panic. "We should have brought her out with us."

"She'll be all right," said Jonah. But I felt no confidence in that. She was now totally unprotected. They would put the pieces together and figure out that I had worked with her.

"How did you get that soft job?" Jonah looked at me keenly. "How did you avoid getting killed on the march to Transnistria?"

"I should rather have been killed than to endure what I did," I said.

"So you nursed Nazis? And Iron Guard?"

"I did worse than that." Both partisans were silent. "Yes, I saved the lives of our enemies. I was good at it, too."

"We do what we must to survive," said Schmuel. "Now you can redeem yourself."

I nodded slowly. But Jonah was not done with me yet. "How could you nurse them? Didn't you want to kill them instead?"

I reached into my pocket and pulled out the scalpel. "They brought in the soldier who murdered my mother and brother in front of my eyes. This was for him," I said. "Or for myself. I hadn't decided."

"Would you have killed him?"

"I don't know. I . . . didn't have a chance."

"Ha ha!" said Schmuel. "You had the chance, all right, you just didn't know how to use it. We'll train you up, don't worry."

"You'll have plenty *not* to tell your grandchildren," said Jonah. The two found this funny and laughed roughly. I was to learn that there were no niceties and courtesies among the partisans. I would be taken to task frequently for being the major's bedmate—until I proved myself and earned respect from them. I remembered how Mihail had comforted me when I told him about being the whore of an Iron Guard officer.

"There is nothing to forgive," Mihail had said. He told me I was as pure to him as the Rose of Sharon. That meant everything. Perhaps someday I could forgive myself. And meanwhile, spending my time reproaching myself would only distract me and impair my effectiveness as a fighter.

A Warrior Is Born

WE FINALLY ARRIVED at an encampment deep in the forest. Our partisan cell consisted of both Soviets and Jews. Schmuel had warned me that some of the Russians were anti-Semites, but our common purpose was gradually breaking down the hate they had been raised with. Our cell consisted of twenty-nine Soviet partisans and thirty Jews fighting side by side, and we were part of an extensive network of clandestine groups spread out across the villages.

At the news of Mihail's death, both the Russians and the Jews mourned and grieved. He had been an indispensable soldier and operative, one of the most capable in the entire region. Everyone knew that he had been my lover, and I received more than a few bitter looks.

"You realize," said a Russian unexpectedly one day, "that Mihail volunteered for the mission in order to bring you out."

"I didn't know that," I said. "I wish it had been I who was killed instead of him." The Russian shrugged. "I realize that every person here agrees. It doesn't hurt me to know that."

"A woman is very valuable out here," said the Russian.

"Especially one like you, strong and not bad looking. You must have given Mihail a good time or two."

"Believe me that I did," I said, and suddenly we both laughed.

"At least he died a happy man," said the Russian. "Plenty of men would trade their lives for love these days." He looked at me keenly. "I know I would."

"Forget it," I said. "That part of my life is over."

Now he laughed hard. "Oh, I don't think so, not by a mile."

"My life means nothing to me now."

The Russian sighed. "Then you have plenty of company. I lost my brothers and my parents. I am alone in the world. Millions of us are. We have to build a new life somehow if we live through the war. Right now I live only to kill Germans. That comforts me. When I kill a German soldier, I tell my mother in heaven it was for her. And she blesses me."

So little by little I made friends among the others. I proved that I was a willing, competent fighter, and my nursing skills were valued. We all had a common purpose and needed one another. Eventually I made love with the Russian boy and with Schmuel and Jonah as well. The soul and the body have their needs, and we didn't deny them.

I learned that there were other units working even farther behind the German lines, and these relied on us to be cohesive and efficient. There were propaganda efforts going on all the time as well, trying to convince Romanian soldiers to desert, or to turn their weapons against Antonescu and Hitler.

One of our ongoing duties was to build up weapons

caches by gathering materiel abandoned on the battle-fields. When the Nazis had first invaded Russia, the Red Army, unprepared and undersupplied, had had to retreat before their attacks, taking heavy casualties. So the Russians had cached weapons throughout the countryside, and it was our duty to retrieve these and make them available to other partisan units as well as our own.

Weapons were as precious as life itself. Even during the melée of our first mission, the partisans had managed to snatch up a few extra guns and ammunition from the major's stock in his room.

Currently, we had forty-four rifles, sixty-three grenades, three machine gun belts, and five-hundred-sixty rounds of ammunition. There were also twenty revolvers, two assault rifles, and one carbine. My first training was to learn how to service and clean weapons, assemble and disassemble them. I learned how to do that blindfolded, just by the feel of the various parts. The guns became like personal companions to me; each had its own idiosyn-crasies, strengths, and weaknesses.

Healing Under Fire

IF I HAD NEVER known Mihail, I sometimes think, my life could have taken me on Jonah's route. At times like this I conjure up my friend Priva, as alive and full of mischief as she always was despite her conservative and proper Jewish upbringing.

I look deep into the forest now, and I see again the conspiratorial glint in her eyes as we talked about our favorite books—about Fitzgerald and Hemingway's Paris in the 1920s and what fun we would have had living there as shameless flappers. And about our mutual crush on Lady Chatterley's gamekeeper lover, the sexually agile Mellors. We used to imagine the moves he would make and sometimes even try them out on each other, one playing Mellors and one Connie, and then changing roles, laughing with our faces buried in the pillows. Yes, we did that, and I feel no shame at our girlish experiments after the brutality and outrage I have witnessed and endured. Prudery is for a different world than this one.

"What about Jonah then?" I would ask Priva's hovering shade, restored and brimming with life. And she would reply to me in a clear and audible voice, the music of which I heard so vividly in my brain that I can only agree with those physicists who tell us that everything in the universe is conserved and never disappears but only takes another form.

"He's attractive," Priva would say to me, "but not the man for you, not for the life ahead."

"If I even have a life," I always added, preemptively, to ward off disaster.

"He is perfect for a wartime fling. But he doesn't think of himself in that way. He takes himself very seriously. He is a very moral man, with all his prayers and laws—many of them aimed at keeping women pure enough to qualify for a man's lust."

"I think the word for him is inhibited," I said to her. "A pity."

"Inhibited is an understatement," Priva replied.

"Although inhibitions can be gotten over, as Mihail proved to me."

"His task was not so difficult," Priva giggled. "You were an apt pupil. But Jonah doesn't want to walk free. He truly believes in all those Jewish prohibitions and traditional rites—to him the life of a happy Jew is rituals and holidays and study and prayer. And that is what he would be doing now if he were not killing Nazis. It's what he lives to do in Israel someday. If he lives."

"Still, Jonah is rather impressive, sometimes," I said. "He tells me that strong young people like us are needed to build the Jewish homeland that is surely coming."

"You would have done that with Mihail," Priva reminded me. "Don't forget. I can see into your thoughts."

"Yes. But without Mihail, I have no path after the war. I live from day to day. I go where fate propels me. If that happens to be Israel I will go to Israel. But my fate may be death or captivity this very night. So how can I decide?"

"You're your father's daughter. And Mihail's little shameless vixen. Jonah would spend half his time scolding you for being impious. And if there were children . . ."

". . . and I wanted to raise them as socialist atheists . . ."

"You and he would fight. You would call him a superstitious product of the *shtetl* and of oppression."

"Thank you for putting words into my mouth, Priva. In case I ever need them."

And Priva would laugh as she faded away into the dimension she now inhabited. I would sometimes hear her and laugh suddenly at her infectious humor; if somebody was within earshot, they might turn and look at me with concern. I would return their puzzled gaze boldly: Go ahead and stare. Maybe I am insane after all. Do I care what you think of me?

Jonah looked like a publicity poster that the Zionists might circulate when they tried to talk us into emigrating to Eretz Israel when the war ended. A mop of wavy blond hair that he clipped short. Resolute, symmetrical features. One could easily picture him silhouetted against an orange grove, tanned and muscular, his blue eyes bleached by the Middle Eastern sun, clutching his deadly submachine gun, his uniform fitting oh-so-perfectly.

It didn't take us long to become lovers once my initial shock over losing Mihail had settled into the persistent ache I would bear all my life. The body has its own wisdom, its own imperatives. And Jonah was both patient and persistent.

He was as fearless and dedicated a partisan as Mihail must have been. But he brought God with him not only into every battle—but into every meal and every conversation. The prayers and quotations from the Talmud and Jewish teachings were deep in his bones and blood.

"You believe it all," I said to him.

"Every bit. What good does it do to be 'sort of' Jewish or partly Jewish? There is no such thing. If you are a Jew, you are a Jew throughout."

The thought occurred to me that this was precisely what the Nazis had always said, that there was only the binary: Jewish or not-Jewish. That being Jewish is a race and not a religion or set of beliefs. You couldn't shed your Judaism just by denying it.

"So if I am Jewish, then I don't need to believe in the religion at all. I am just as Jewish as you are."

"Let's not talk about this now," Jonah would say gently. "I can teach you why . . ."

"You can *teach* me how to take apart a gun, Jonah, but not how to think. *Meine gedanken sind frei.*"

"Yes, your thoughts are free," Jonah would reply, "but the truths that God gave to the Jews are—"

"Enough!" I would shout. "You are spoiling my romantic mood with these tedious religious arguments. This is not a study house."

"Why do you hate God?"

"Why do you love God?"

"Did you know that in one town the murderers looted the sacred Jewish texts belonging to their victims and tore out the pages to use to wrap fruit in the marketplace?"

"I hope they choked on their fruit."

"But to you those sacred pages have no more meaning than the novels you say you devoured."

"No, they are precious in a historical way, but they

are not the direct word of your God. Because there is no God."

"You are hopeless, Daniela."

"Then give up on me. You will never put me in the wig of a dutiful Jewish *balabosta*." And I tossed my thick rebellious head of hair, also clipped short now to discourage lice.

He took my face in his hands and kissed me. "Your love of arguing is proof enough of your Judaism." He laughed.

But the thought of the synagogue's precious, ancient texts used to wrap fruit for the greedy slobbering mouths of vicious killers would not leave me alone. I thought of Papa's old student books and Torah gathering dust behind his desk. How I would have loved to have that scroll with me now. But I would never confess that to Jonah.

"Your father's atheism and Communism are every bit as much a religion as my Judaism," Jonah said to me more than once.

"And if my father ever saw scientific evidence that refuted his beliefs, he would abandon them. If he saw some proof that God existed he would leave his atheism behind. But there is no proof. There were never any miracles. Not a single one since the beginning of time. God is a human construct."

"And you have been around to observe all this . . ."

Jonah and I lay side by side. I knew that my arguing had dampened his desire for me. And I felt guilty that I resented his faith. How deep did my anger and bitterness go? How warped was I by what I had endured? Was I blaming Judaism itself for our sufferings?

"Jonah," I said, quietly now, "would you teach me

the letters of the Hebrew alphabet?" He looked up and grinned as if he had found a spark in a cold fireplace.

"If you're sure the integrity of your atheism won't be polluted," he teased. "I will teach you the language that we have preserved over thousands of years. The killers can tear up the pages of our sacred texts, but they cannot erase the knowledge that we Jews hold in our minds." He reached for me and kissed me lovingly, and I felt the traitorous tears welling in my eyes, and he kissed them away and we made love at last, two orphans.

During my time with the Russian partisans, we set ablaze a German fuel depot, destroying hundreds of oil barrels and nearly thirty gasoline tank cars. Our primary targets were the Germans' railroads because their supply lines were long and weak, running deep into Soviet territory and giving us many great opportunities to destroy tracks.

Another Russian partisan group caused two major train collisions and also took down a railway bridge while setting fire to cars that were bringing fodder and military equipment to the German troops. I was amazed to learn that partisans had destroyed a whole meat processing plant, and two electrical substations, plus burning a grain warehouse, and local oil and cheese factories.

The German defeat at Stalingrad was really the turning point in the war, breaking the back of Germany once and for all, but the fighting and killing and dying and suffering went on for years before Germany could be brought crashing down.

We were a part of that. Following Stalingrad, the number of partisan groups multiplied. People were realizing that the Nazis were on the run at last, and the links among the partisan networks were strengthened and increased by local folk who now came out of hiding and joined up. Everyone was getting aboard the final push to the west.

As the Red Army now went on the offensive, additional leaders came to help command Bessarabian partisans like us. Thanks to our work, many Romanians saw the writing on the wall and switched sides, joining the Red Army and the partisans.

The Germans soon realized to their detriment that the forests of Bessarabia and Transnistria were full of partisans—we were even reinforced by Soviet paratroopers and airdropped supplies.

"It's time to celebrate," Jonah said to me one morning. "Soviet forces have conquered Romania, and Antonescu has been arrested. Eichmann never reached Romania to organize the liquidation of our people. Mihail was a part of bringing that about."

"That's great news," I said, "but who is Eichmann going after now that he can't reach the Romanian Jews?"

"Probably the Hungarians," Jonah said. "They are at terrible risk." And so they were. I later learned over 440,000 Jews who had fled to Hungary thinking they might be safe there were deported to Auschwitz and murdered in the gas chambers. This even as Hitler's entire Third Reich was collapsing in fire and blood—losing hundreds of thousands of men on the retreat from Russia while their waiting families and children were incinerated under the relentless fire bombings.

I learned later that Ileana was betrayed and tortured to death after the partisan attack. But the Iron Guard monster who murdered my mother and brother made a full recovery. There is no justice in this world; perhaps there is in the next, but I don't believe in an afterlife.

Social Calls from the Supernatural

"YOU NEED TO SLEEP," Jonah said; it was a command, not an affectionate reminder. I had been sitting apart, turned away from the fire, and staring into the darkness. The trees reassured me; I would think about their roots reaching strong and deep into the soil seeking nourishment, carrying the nutritious sap upward to the branches, sustaining life year after year. The lives of us humans were so stunted and temporary; we were so vulnerable, I was thinking. But the trees endured and spread their branches, producing their leaves and seeds and fruit; sustained and protected other living things. . . .

"Did you hear me? What are you looking at? Do you see something out there?"

I wouldn't have told him, but I did indeed see things. My old fear of madness, never far, had returned, but this time I was embracing the idea. I had begun sensing—and sometimes even glimpsing—spirits among us, here in the woods.

At first I had scolded myself that they were a hallucination or an illusion of the flickering fire. I had looked away, occupying myself with some chore or starting up a conversation. But soon, I began to sit apart, opening up my eyes and mind, beckoning the spirits or demons or golems—whatever they were. I didn't fear the unliving anymore. After all, the people I loved and trusted the most were no longer living. And what demon could commit any act more evil and cruel than I had witnessed humans do to each other? So I let my curiosity wander among the forest, come what may.

Perhaps my senses were just overwrought, my tormented imagination was reacting to the horrors I had seen and endured. But what if it was not? What if the dead had only assumed another form and were reaching out to whoever was open to encounter them? There were so many; the sheer mass of those who had departed their bodies could have generated some mysterious force beyond our senses. Would millions of souls just lie quietly and invisibly forever? That didn't seem possible.

I had glanced through my father's scientific tracts and books. I knew that physicists—the most brilliant people in the world—believed the information that lived in our brain resided in the atoms that composed it. The electrons and forces within each tiny atom were unimaginably powerful and as old as time itself.

Something that had once existed, said my father's books, could not simply become nothing. It could only change its form. So our dead bodies rotted and became part of the soil; we all knew that. And our brains were only three pounds of "pudding" as my father called it. But that flesh was always seething with electrons, and those electrons had to go somewhere when the heart stopped beating, when the physical brain could no longer host them.

We had heard that American and British planes were firebombing German cities now at will, without pause, reducing them to rubble and ash, incinerating the people, whether they were Nazis or newborns. But what if even a firebomb was not destructive enough? What if the evil that was Germany survived and re-armed yet again?

My father had told me that scientists were seeking ways to unleash the forces inside the atom and turn them into a super-weapon that could vaporize whole nations. I believed him. I could only hope that the Americans were ahead in the race to harness the atom. I knew that the Germans were desperately trying to build such a super-weapon, now that they were losing the war. Was that not a more frightening prospect than a mere imp in the forest?

"Come closer," I whispered to one of the shapes I saw slipping from tree to tree as if teasing me. When I tried to focus on the thing, it dodged my eyes and reappeared a few feet away. It was completely transparent, and yet I could see it. An outline defined it, but it had no substance within. How was that possible?

"Are you talking to yourself?" Jonah's voice came to me again.

"I am talking to the dead," I whispered back.

"Then you are going off your head."

"Why? You talk to a God that never existed. Why can't I talk to people who actually once had bodies and minds and voices?"

"I have something you can come talk to."

I drowsed and awoke suddenly to a voice in my head: "Hello, Daniela," it greeted me in Russian, the voice of a friendly young man. I spoke little Russian; I was trying to learn as fast as I could because I needed to converse with the Russian partisans and peasants.

"Who . . . are you?" I whispered in Russian.

"I am Alyosha. From Ukraine."

"I am dreaming you."

"If you say so."

I raised myself on one elbow and looked around but saw nobody. I turned over and tried to go back to sleep, but I felt a presence somewhere close by.

"What do you want with me?"

"I get lonely. Is it allowed?"

"How did you die?" I asked. Because I knew that this was not a living soul.

"I starved to death in 1933. My last meal was a toad my father found in the marsh. We all died in Stalin's famine, so that he could export the wheat we grew to England, where nobody was even hungry, ha ha. Stalin wanted to prove that Communism and his collective farms in Ukraine were making Russia prosperous. He wanted to play the hero."

"Stalin is leading Russia to victory," I said.

"Do you think that excuses his crimes? Perhaps it does," Alyosha said. "My father was a *Kulak*, a private farmer. We were not wealthy, but we never went hungry, and we even had a few luxuries. This made us Stalin's enemies. He wanted us to turn over all of our animals and seed and implements to the collective and then work for it. The very things we owned were no longer ours. We objected to that, so Stalin set out to destroy us."

"My father was a Communist," I whispered, "but he didn't object to my mama making money by tailoring dresses for the aristocrats."

"Ha!" said Alyosha. "Some Communist he was!" I laughed softly but affectionately, thinking of my papa and his mischievous brown eyes and his beard.

"We had a beautiful little farm," said Alyosha. "The land had been in our family for a hundred years and more. The earth was so rich and fertile that you could watch the wheat grow. One minute you would plant, you would turn your back for a few hours, and when you looked again, the wheat was waving in the wind."

"They came and took everything. All the food we had hidden. Whatever we buried, they found it anyway. They tore up the floorboards of our house. We had not a crumb left, not one seed. We knew that in other parts of Russia people had enough to eat. The famine was only for Ukraine. But Stalin would not allow food to be shipped in to us kulaks. Not a morsel. My younger sister and brother and my mother all starved."

"I lost my whole family," I said. "The Iron Guard shot . . ."

"We ate their corpses after they died, my father and I. We thought they would want us to live. But then we died, too, anyway."

I shook my head in disbelief. With all the horrors I had seen and heard, this was something new.

"I would die myself before I became a cannibal. . . ."

"That's what you say, Daniela. We were good people. Our neighbors killed and ate their baby. We would not have done that."

"I don't know what's true anymore."

"Everything is true."

"Daniela," came Jonah's voice, sharply now, "go to sleep. You're babbling in Russian. I worry about you."

"I don't speak Russian," I said.

"All I know is you are waking me. Come over and keep me warm."

At 4:00 A.M., we rose and quietly separated into twos and threes. Our target was a storage depot outside a tiny village near Minsk, where the Germans had received casks of cooking oil to fry their meals.

Fat was a very precious substance. Everybody was at risk of what they called rabbit starvation or rabbit hunger: there was meat to be trapped here in the woods; we could catch rodents and even deer, but the meat was leathery and tough and had only a little fat in the bone marrow. Without fat, you starve, even when your belly is full. The meat becomes a sort of poison. Sometimes you go insane. Rabbit starvation is not pleasant. So oil of any kind was precious; we were crazy for it. I would sit and think about the dripping roasts and briskets my mother cooked, the chicken skin oozing savory grease. I used to peel the chicken and eat only the meat because I didn't want to get fat. Now my ribs protruded, and my hipbones were sharp.

The peasants nearby had already given the Russian partisans all they could spare, and the Russians shared it with us Jews, but grudgingly. Everyone was hungry all the time, including the Germans. That was a comfort to me. They could not get their supply flights past the Russian air force anymore by now; their Luftwaffe was so diminished that they could not defend their cities against the relentless waves of American and British bombers, let alone haul supplies out to their starving soldiers in the east. And of course, destroying railroad tracks was one of our most important missions. Anything that could disconnect the Germans from their ammunition and food was our target.

Whenever a German supply plane was shot down, peasants would rush out and grab everything. The Germans sent their soldiers all kinds of tidbits and packages, wrapped with loving hands, like knitted sweaters and chocolates. We tore up the photographs that were included in the packages and threw them to the wind, smiling *Frauen*—wives—and *kinder*, the plump blond German babies of the murderers. Nobody was starving there. The Germans had looted all of the countries they conquered and brought back food and everything of value to Germany. Trains carried off the possessions of millions of families.

Now, I liked the idea of German soldiers starving and wasting away here in the east. We knew they had had a very bad time since Stalingrad. The Russians showed German prisoners little mercy, just as the Germans had let their Russian prisoners starve after they invaded Russia. This war blazed new trails in brutality.

How Far Can I Go?

"WAKE UP, DANIELA!" Jonah was shaking me. "Come see the *Schmeissers*." He was so excited that his usually taciturn features were glowing with joy.

"*Schmeissers?*"

"We got a couple of them. Come see. And bullets!" He sounded as though he was welcoming surprise guests for dinner.

I rose and went into the woods to relieve myself while Jonah waited impatiently. The woods were soaking in a sudden light rain, the sun was a mere light spot like a pale button on the horizon, nearly invisible through the dark, roiling clouds. More rain must be on the way.

The *Schmeissers*, legendary submachine weapons, and a couple of handguns, too, were stacked near the cooking fire. Breakfast was already well underway, a mixture of groats and who-knew-what-else.

At the fire were two other women who had recently joined our group, a young girl like myself called Mira, with curly black hair, deep brown eyes, and a flushed, rosy complexion. The other, a blonde woman in her early thirties, was named Vitka. She had been a society matron in Poland, married to a gentile man who was a professor of medieval literature in a university. She had made it to our group by some impossible route that had led her across Europe, using her ability to speak fluent German to pass as a gentile and flirt her way through checkpoints.

Vitka had been separated from her two children by the Nazis after they invaded Poland. And her husband had scurrilously renounced her in order to save himself and his professorship. The children, nine and thirteen, were considered *"mischlings"*—mixed race Jewish and gentile. But they were declared officially Jewish, of course, because their mother was a Jew, and anyway, half Jewish was all Jewish to the Germans. So was a quarter Jewish. And an eighth, and less than that. So Vitka's children had no chance; the Germans deported them to Treblinka. But Vitka had somehow escaped from the train. She told us that the Germans had murdered her husband anyway, along with many other thousands of Polish intellectuals. So he died not for being a Jew but for being a Pole. Go figure.

Vitka was hefting one of the *Schmeissers* with reverence. "It fires five hundred rounds a minute," Jonah was saying, "across two hundred meters. What we can do with this!" But it was another automatic weapon that he was really impressed with: they were calling it a "Sarc."

"To lose one of these," Jonah said, "is a court martial offense for a German."

"What unlucky bastard lost it?" I laughed. "And how did they get . . ." Jonah jerked his head left, and I stopped talking because I saw two battered German soldiers tied with their backs to a tree. The Russians had captured them in some sortie last night and brought them back alive. The partisans now stood encircling the two, staring as if at some strange creatures that had crawled up from the bowels of the earth.

"Behold," Jonah said, and then he said something in Hebrew.

I gawked. These very young men were both ordinary soldiers, not officers, not SS. They had been captured while taking a pee and knocked unconscious. Now they were awakening to find themselves prisoners of the Soviets—and the Jews.

At first I laughed. "What a beautiful sight!" But Jonah was looking at me meaningfully and seriously.

"Do you recall what we said when we were escaping in the truck from the Hotin Legion headquarters and leaving Mihail dead in the woods?"

I nodded. "We said a lot of things."

"Do you recall that we said we would teach you how to kill? After you missed the opportunity to kill the murderer of your mother and brother?"

"What do you mean?"

"You have had a comparatively easy time, Daniela. It's time for you to take a life. Choose one of them and shoot him."

"No," quickly interjected one of the Russians, "we cannot waste bullets to make it easy on your little . . ." he paused, searching for a word ". . . pet. If you want to teach your student here how to kill, she will have to do it the old-fashioned way." He tapped the knife in his belt. "Or you can show her how to do it with her hands."

"Oh no," I gasped. I suddenly thought of cheetahs in Africa who brought home helpless young antelopes still alive so that they could teach their cubs to hunt and kill. A wave of horror washed over me.

The Germans were looking at their captors—and at me, of course. I think they guessed what was being said. They knew they were doomed, and it would do absolutely no good to plead for their lives or try to talk their way out of captivity. All they could hope for was a merciful and quick death, and now they were not to get even that.

"This is ridiculous," said the Russian. "Take them down now or else we will do it."

"I . . . I cannot murder . . . in cold blood," I blurted.

"Then you are no good to us, and you might even get us killed," Jonah said. "You want others to do the dirty work. You have to prove that you are willing to take the ultimate step. Are you one of us or not?"

The Russian took out his knife and put it in my hand. "Go on. Hurry up."

"It's one thing to defend yourself," I said. "But . . ."

"Daniela," Jonah said, "do it now. Because your yammering only prolongs their suffering. We can't feed them or take them with us. We certainly can't turn them loose. Think of your dead family. Think of your friend Priva. And think of Mihail. You were a nurse—you know better than we do where the vital organs are. Now go over there and do your duty."

I choked and began to cry. "Don't make me," I said. "I cannot." Everybody moved away from us, and the thought struck me what a sick lover's quarrel this was. I think Jonah sensed he was losing status from my defiance of him, my weakness.

"Oh Christ," Jonah said finally as I sobbed. I had never seen him so angry. He grabbed the knife dangling from my limp hand and strode over to the Germans. They started to protest, but he butchered them both as quickly and efficiently as if he were slaughtering a lamb for the table. Even the Russians were a little amazed at how fast it went.

He walked back to me, stuck the knife into the wet earth several times to clean it, and handed it back to the Russian, who nodded his thanks. But people do not die obediently and quickly. Everybody turned their faces away from the death throes, but Jonah did not. He stood close and watched the Germans die because, as he later said, it was important to take ownership of your deed. The partisans burned the Germans' identity cards and the contents of their wallets, including photos of smiling relatives.

After this episode Jonah did not speak to me for a long time. I knew that I disappointed him in so many ways. Sometimes he was merry and sarcastic, and we laughed together, but I couldn't help feeling that I was only a stopgap of a kind in his life, a woman who satisfied his physical needs but whose mind and soul were on a different plane entirely.

Amid all of the horrors and uncertainty, singing was the sweetest joy and comfort to us all; on cold, hungry nights, the Russians would sing their melancholy traditional songs, and we Jews sang, too, to keep our spirits up:

Never say that you are going your last way.
Though lead-filed skies blot out the blue of day.
The earth shall thunder 'neath our tread that
    we are here.
The hour for which we long will certainly appear.
From lands of green palm trees to lands all white
    with snow,

The Dressmaker's Daughter

we are coming with our pain and with our woe.
And wherever a spurt of our blood did drop,
our courage will again sprout from that spot.
For us the morning sun will radiate the day.
The enemy and past will fade away.

But should the dawn delay or sunrise wait too long,
then like a codeword let all generations sing this song.
This song was written with our blood and
   not with lead.
This is no song of free birds flying overhead.
But a people amid crumbling walls did stand,
they stood and sang this song with pistols
   held in hand.

So never say that you are going your last way.
Though lead-filled skies blot out the blue of day.
The hour that we long for will certainly appear.
The earth shall thunder 'neath our tread that
   WE ARE HERE.

Embracing the Departed

WHY THEN, I asked myself, if I was to be visited by the spirits of the dead in dark of night, could Mihail not be among them? Why could he not find his way to me? Because Alyosha was only the first of several souls who began to appear when I was half asleep. Sometimes they were troubled women who had lost children or pregnancies and were seeking the beloved departed. Once a murderer came to me and whispered his confession in my always-waiting ear. He had killed his cheating business partner in a paper factory in Odessa in 1913, he told me, although from the way he described the situation, it sounded to me as though he himself was the actual embezzler.

At first I told myself that my fevered imagination and the trauma of losing my family and Mihail had triggered a delusional state; perhaps the psychosis I had always suspected of lurking in my mind was manifesting at last, and this was how my life would be from now on. I would be one of those unfortunate people who actually believes in the reality of their delusions. If not killed in the war, I would end up in a mental institution, perhaps with a lobotomy, a compliant vegetable.

I did not dare tell Jonah of these episodes. Out of courtesy toward the single men in our group and for the sake of morale, I kept to myself and only made love with Jonah when the others were away or asleep. We were very quiet at those times. Otherwise, we slept apart, although nobody was really fooled. Jonah said that flaunting our relationship in front of a group of men who were facing death the next morning could goad one of them to rape, and then the cohesion of our group would be shattered. We had to keep the common good of the group uppermost and above our desire for each other. So the one thing that could have kept the *dybbuks* away—a man in my arms—was not available to me.

Because I had decided that the visitors were *dybbuks*. The very creatures that Papa and I used to laugh about, they were so unlikely, just a product of ancient superstitions. But now I was able to see them better, dressed sometimes in long caftans and fur hats and collars. Other times they wore old-fashioned Russian uniforms from the days of the Czar or dressed like Cossacks.

Alyosha the Ukrainian never came back, nor did the embezzling murderer of his partner, but a man named Seryozha actually tried to make love to me. He was a Cossack who had been killed in 1857 in a skirmish in the Caucasus Mountains, a very minor skirmish, and his wound had not been severe, he told me, but inexplicably, they had been unable to stop his bleeding, and so he had died anyway in the evening, with many people wringing their hands at his bedstead.

"The town girls were devastated," Seryozha told me, and I actually felt a sort of heat emanating from him. "I was tall and very handsome. I can say this now truthfully since there is no need to deceive in our sphere."

"Why must men constantly battle one another?" I asked him.

"To prove ourselves, to prevail. What other way is there?"

"What a question!" I said. "There are a thousand ways to achieve distinction besides wounding or killing another man."

"But nothing has the glory of warfare," Seryozha replied. "Well, perhaps sports like fencing and steeplechase ... but to risk one's life and vanquish a mortal enemy ... to show daring and courage and reckless disregard for one's safety—ah, that's what life is all about."

"That didn't work out very well for you, though, did it?"

"I was a great lover," Seryozha said, unruffled by my arguments. And then he actually reached out and touched me; I suddenly felt his lips at my ear, and a shiver ran over my entire body.

"I could have you in a trice," Seryozha said. "You would be my easiest conquest ever."

"Leave me alone," I hissed. "I am damaged goods, and anyway my body belongs to another."

"And how many 'others' has it belonged to, eh?" Suddenly, I felt him running his hands over me, touching my breasts lightly. He was everywhere, and I became helpless under his touch. "I enjoy giving pleasure," Seryozha said as I lay shuddering, trying not to cry out. "It is all that is left to me. Perhaps I will visit you tomorrow night, too. You are a welcome diversion in this bleak eternity." And he was gone, leaving me alone and stunned. What now was to become of me? This was unquestionably insanity taking hold. "Oh, Mihail," I breathed, "if I'm to be insane, why can't it at least be you who accompanies me over the edge?"

I later found out from Vitka that the Russians were making bets as to who would have me after Jonah tired of me. They had heard me whispering to Seryozha even though I believed I spoke only a smattering of Russian I had picked up. They said I was speaking in full sentences, and worse, they had understood some of my whisperings.

People thought I was an odd duck, Vitka told me, but they didn't dislike me because my experience at the Romanian field hospital had made me skilled at nursing and at dressing wounds. I was a hard worker, and a strong-willing woman was always in demand for washing and cooking and cleaning. We tried to keep our campsite clean and not to soil or pollute the earth.

Mira had fallen in love with one of the Russian partisans, and had turned up pregnant, which was my own biggest fear. A peasant woman had given her some herbs intended to terminate the pregnancy, but the father, a strapping blond Slavic-looking Russian partisan youth named Yevgeny, had found out and confronted her and thrown them away. He wanted the baby, even amid hardship and war, the urge to live endured.

Mira had been trained in classical piano and also had a beautiful singing voice. Yevgeny would listen to her and the tears would roll unabashedly down his cheeks. His family had been murdered by the Nazis in the first wave of Operation Barbarossa in 1941. Advance German forces had roared into Yevgeny's village, where the family was celebrating a Russian holiday, and his mother had been cooking and baking for days.

When the Nazis arrived, they had immediately killed Yevgeny's parents, his heavily pregnant sister, and her husband, Yevgeny's childhood friend. Yevgeny, who had been out hauling water from the river, had returned to find his family dead and German soldiers eagerly sitting down to eat the family's meal amid the carnage. Unnoticed, he had escaped and eventually made his way to the partisans. I saw how tenderly he would speak with Mira and how reverently he would touch her, and I thought of Mihail. Jonah never showed such affection toward me. I think a part of him envied Mihail because my heart belonged only to him. I was removed—alienated—from my body; how else could I have survived the death march and the rapes and my nights with Major Dragulescu?

The Russian army had taken terrible losses in the early days, and they continued to worsen as the war dragged on. Stalin spent lives like a rich man spent rubles. All that mattered was to push the Germans relentlessly westward, toward Berlin, to bleed them dry.

I knew that Operation Barbarossa, the initial German invasion, had caught Russia and Stalin unprepared. In the early days, the Germans had swept toward Moscow, paced by speeding tanks and a sky dark with planes.

So Russian soldiers had been captured in massive hordes and nearly all of these were doomed. But the difference was, there were many more Russians to take their place, whereas the Nazis now began to take casualties that their smaller population could not replace. There were simply not enough young men. There were not enough natural resources or food in Germany to resupply and support the invading German armies throughout the vast expanses of Russia.

So the initial invasion had bogged down deep in Russian territory, and the Germans had changed strategy. Now they were trying desperately to take the oilfields at Baku. That was doomed to failure, too.

The Russian partisans told us how the retreating Russian army in the early days of the invasion had cached weapons and food as they fell back before the Germans, retreating and drawing the Germans deeper and deeper into the limitless Russian expanses as winter approached. The German supply lines grew longer and longer—which meant weaker and more vulnerable to explosives and partisan attacks.

The Russians knew that someday they would return across these lands; they would reconquer this terrain and chase the German army back to Berlin, as they were now doing. The Red Army soon realized what a priceless resource their partisans were and began to airdrop supplies and weapons. And of course we Jews who fought alongside them benefited as well.

Romania finally signed a separate peace in 1944 and entered the war on the side of the Allies. The Jewish agencies were then allowed to come in and rescue the fragments of our people who were left.

An Improbable Future

"DANIELA," Jonah said to me as we two sat before a tiny fire, "you have to make a decision. The war will soon end, and you are a stateless person. The International Red Cross is trying to persuade the Romanians to allow Jews to emigrate to Palestine. Of course you can return to Romania legally now, if you wish."

"Never," I said.

"Many of the Jews who were deported to Transnistria are actually going back to their homes. There is still a life to be had, perhaps."

"Not for me."

"I knew as much."

"Everyone I loved is dead. The Daniela who lived there is dead as well. I cannot return to Yedinitz. It is a cursed place. I would see in every street the murderers and plunderers of my family and our people."

"But you would also see other Jews . . ."

"I wish them well. I don't understand them, but they somehow still think Romania is home."

"The Zionists are building a whole new Jewish life in our biblical homeland. The American government is pressuring Romania to allow survivors of the

Transnistrian Death March to go to Palestine. They are asking the British government to stop trying to keep the Jews out."

"What about the people living in those Palestinian territories now? Will they simply pack up and depart as Jews take over their homes?"

"It's desert, much of it."

"Have you seen it with your own eyes? And what if it is desert? People can still consider the desert home."

Jonah put his head in his hands. "Think of your people, Daniela. Haven't we suffered enough?"

"Jonah, I know what it's like to be evicted from my home and deported. How could I be a part of deporting others? Even with the best reasons, we would still be displacing people...."

"Do you not believe in Israel, in the Jewish homeland? After what you've been through?"

"I do. But how can we build peace on the—"

"The Jews have occupied those lands since biblical times. There is even an old Romanian Jewish colony living in Israel now."

"So the Bible is dispensing land now, from thousands of years ago? Who are those sages that understand what people need in 1945?"

"But where will you go? You will be put into a Displaced Persons camp...."

"Yes," I said, "I've heard about those. Maybe I can find myself somewhere else. I don't know."

"I'm offering you the opportunity to come to Palestine with me. Daniela, do you ... can you love me even a little?"

"It's because I do love you that I can't go with you,

Jonah. I am not the partner you need. You need some-body who believes in Zionism and is willing to live and die for it. And to spend their whole lives in what I think will become an endless war."

"I am willing to fight and die for Israel. I can think of nothing sweeter than to build the Jewish homeland. Daniela, Daniela, you are a lost soul."

I took him in my arms. "I know that you will find the right partner in Eretz Israel, Jonah. Somebody who be-lieves in your God and your religious traditions and ob-servances. I can't be that person. Especially after what I have seen and been through. I would have to give up my own independence of mind and spirit that my father in-stilled in me; to become somebody other than who I am. My life would be a charade. I would go through the mo-tions of religious observance that are so much a part of you, so meaningful to you. But for me, the life would be empty, all lies."

"You don't know that. You might find your faith."

"I hope I never do. I would lose myself."

Tears filled Jonah's eyes. "Daniela, I will never forget you. I will love you until the day I die."

"And I will love you too, Jonah."

A Welcome from the Past

I LEARNED LATER that thousands of Jews eventually emigrated to Palestine from Romania. Jonah was among them, I'm sure. I'll never know if he made it after reading of those notoriously dangerous passages in which casualties from sinking boats reached the thousands. I only hope he found the life he had earned so bravely.

But of all the alternatives I turned over in my mind, going to America was never one of them; it seemed such a remote chance as to be totally impossible. Yet, that was actually how a new life began for me.

When the war ended, I was still in my teens. I had resigned myself to being transported to a Displaced Persons camp with other survivors. I actually found myself arriving by train in the Buchenwald Displaced Persons Camp! Yes! They established a refuge in the same location as the notorious concentration camp. The Zionists even set up "Kibbutz Buchenwald" where Jews were trained in agriculture to prepare for life in Palestine!

There were many people working through agencies trying to find and reunite victims with their families—if any had survived. But I had nobody to search for. My family and friends had all been killed, most of them in front of my eyes. I could search for them only in my heart.

I wandered about the camp lonely and isolated. After the excitement, risk, and sense of purpose I had had as a partisan, the thought of now having plenty of food to eat, a relatively clean place to sleep, and safe surroundings only left me feeling empty, lonely, and dismal. My senses, trained to a fine, keen point to sense danger, now only tormented me amid the constant noise and conversations.

I began to ruminate on the various actions we had taken, going over the details again and again in my mind, looking back nostalgically, as if I had enjoyed them. I wanted to blurt out to people who I was, what I had done, but everybody else was full of the same needs, and their desperate searches for loved ones obsessed them.

Even then, the enormous actuality of the Holocaust and the sheer number of souls who had been killed was hardly appreciated. Statistics were still being tallied, and they seemed beyond comprehension. We could not believe the early estimates that millions and millions of Jews had been murdered in such a mere few years. Not to mention homosexuals, gypsies, the infirm, the mentally ill . . . It seemed impossible. And new facts and horrors kept emerging; the truth kept getting worse. Just when you thought you had heard everything your sanity could bear, new reports of atrocities came in to dwarf what you already knew.

As I dragged myself through the days in uncertainty and isolation, I had all but forgotten about Philippa. But she had been, as I later learned, searching for me tirelessly and with what she later called "insane determination and obsession."

She refused to believe that I had been killed. "It never

entered my mind," she told me. "I knew you would some-how muddle through. I had to believe you were alive in order to feel alive myself! Every day was a fresh opportunity to find you: 'This will be the day; today is the day,' I kept thinking. And one day, it was true!"

So I found myself on a transport to London, crossing the Channel, seasick, numb with cold, and half-starved. But when I landed at Dover, there was my Philippa, as beautiful as ever. The moment we laid eyes on one another, I felt carried back across the years to the orchard behind my home in Yedinitz.

We might as well have been sitting on the wooden bench under a plum tree, gossiping about Countess Kányádi, about men and love and trading stories of Mihail.

"We have so much to catch up on," were her first words to me. And "My God, you're so thin!" quickly followed by "We'll have to fix that!"

Philippa was still living with the count and countess, still being a nanny to their now rapidly growing children. I insisted that I wanted to live in my own place rather than with them in their townhouse, which had been damaged in a V1 rocket attack. The place was full of carpenters and constant activity, and I felt I wanted to be alone with my memories. So they finally stopped protesting and found me a flat in a working class neighborhood called Kentish Town. I couldn't wait to find myself a job and start paying my own way. Even though they were generous, I couldn't bear the idea of taking money from people who were now themselves having to watch their budgets.

My landlady was a friendly, gossipy widow who let out a tiny, detached building to me behind her home, with a real bed and a hot plate to cook my meals. Despite the peeling wallpaper and warped floor, I felt incredibly, luxuriously pampered and fortunate.

Even though I didn't have paper credentials and certification, my battlefield nursing experience stood for me, and I was hired to take care of patients recovering at a convalescent hospital; I was placed under the close supervision of their nursing staff, which I accepted gratefully. I was also able to study English and take training courses in patient care, which seemed unbelievably advanced compared to the Romanian field hospital. Sometimes I thought of how many more lives could have been saved if we had only had half the equipment and resources they had here. I thought back on my dreams of becoming a doctor, but I was still too hard put just to survive—financially and emotionally—to take any action.

After what I had been through I had a lot of trouble adjusting to a land of peace and relative prosperity. Even though there were many shortages and people complained of the rationing, I saw all around me the signs of victory and celebration, only reminding me of how much I had lost. Why could my dear loved ones not have been brought along into this time of peace and hope?

The pubs were full of American servicemen: "Over-sexed, overpaid, and over here" was how their envious British counterparts described the Yanks. People still went about waving British and American flags. They took every opportunity to drink and toast and dance. Parties sprang up spontaneously and lasted all night. Everywhere, people reveled in the luxuries of peace. But among them were the many parents who had lost their sons and widows who had barely had time to marry before being separated forever. Thinking of Mihail and how desperately I had wanted to marry him, I even envied those widows.

As the days passed and the euphoria of my arrival began to turn into daily routine, I learned more from Philippa about her own wartime experiences. She, too, had lost a great love. The man she had fallen for, a pilot, had been killed in a raid over Germany. She had never experienced such deep and helpless grief before, and so she and I now had our lost hopes and stolen moments of happiness in common. We would talk about our men by the hour as if to salve our aching hearts with the sweet memories and laughter.

I told Philippa what had happened to me after she left Yedinitz, glossing over the rapes so she should not feel any worse than she already did about fleeing. She wept for my family and for Mihail. Because she had loved him, too, of course.

The count and countess had lost a lot of their money and property, but they had preserved enough to maintain a life of genteel poverty, living beyond their means and selling off the countess' jewelry and whatever other valuables she had been able to take away from Bessarabia.

"But it's an ill wind . . ." Philippa told me, laughing. "The food rationing during the war was exactly what the countess needed to take off weight. She grew as slender as a girl again and had to have all of your mother's beautiful creations taken in."

War and money worries had aged the count; his elegant tweeds and shoes were worn, and his blond hair had grown thin. He had managed to get the children, Anton and Katerina, into good schools, and any remaining

money they had went to keep up appearances for the
two: riding lessons, coming-out parties, the theater, and
dances.

I Land in a New Life

PHILIPPA AND I had a favorite pub that we frequented. With the Russian partisans I had learned how to drink vodka "neat," as they say, without mixing or diluting it. I laughed at the idea of adding fruit juice or seltzer. We had all passed the jug or bottle, swilling and sharing. But Philippa told me that was one behavior I should discard.

"It will make you look coarse, my darling," she told me, laughing. "And another thing, never drink alone. It's a bad habit."

"It helps me forget," I told her. "It keeps me company." I sometimes sat in my little flat and drank until I fell asleep. Often, I talked to Mihail, but I was alone in my room; his spirit never returned to me. Perhaps it was his way of setting me free. I tried to be quiet, but I suspect my landlady might have heard some of my nighttime babbling.

"And that's precisely why you have to be careful with drink," Philippa said, "and so do I." It was early evening, and we were sitting at a table in the pub. I was still in my nursing uniform drinking a vodka "Collins" as they called it, when Ziggy walked in with a group of American fliers. He did a double take when he saw me—Americans were never subtle about showing what they liked.

I sensed that his interest had a lot to do with my being Jewish, as I could tell he was. So I smiled at him, and he came right over.

"This seat taken?"

"Do you see anybody there?" I answered, but friendly. The other nurses with me and Philippa grinned and made room for him, flirting furiously as he ordered drinks all around, but he never took his eyes off me. He was tall, as all Americans seemed to be, with thick, curly brown hair that was already growing out of its military cut. I felt Philippa's sly elbow dig into my ribs and almost laughed. This was her way of communicating that he was a "catch." His brown eyes were dancing with sexy mischief; he knew he was attractive, and that made him bold.

"So what kind of accent is that?" he asked.

"Romanian," I said. "Yiddish. Maybe a little Russian. You name it."

"You're Jewish then?"

"Does that make a difference?"

"Of course. You had it rough, there in Romania, I heard."

"You heard right. You are a captain?"

"Close enough. I'm a First Lieutenant, and I fly a B-24 Liberator. I should say 'flew.' I'll probably never touch one again."

"And that makes you sad?"

"Are you kidding? I kissed my ass goodbye so many times I lost count."

"Oh. That sounds like a difficult position to assume."

"I wouldn't touch that one with a ten-foot pole."

"What does that mean?" I asked, "ten-foot pole?"

Ziggy looked closely at me. "You're a cheeky one."

"And what means cheeky?"

"Uh . . . I think you need some lessons in American slang," he said, laughing.

"Is that so? You can be my tutor then. Do you have anything else to teach me?"

"Do you learn fast?"

"Faster than you would believe."

Ziggy threw his head back and laughed. "I think you could teach me a few things," he said with a wink and reached his arm around me.

At this, I rose and began to put on my hat.

"Wait, stop!" Ziggy got up and ran after me because I was walking away, my cheeks burning. I was realizing that I still carried around a lot of shame. "I didn't mean to go too far. That's the last thing I meant to do. You'll have to get used to me putting my foot in my mouth."

"Your foot fits in your mouth?"

Once more Ziggy laughed. "Here we go again!"

So I let him bring me back to the bar. Drinks arrived, and Ziggy hoisted his glass.

"Drink to . . . what, Romania?"

"Not as long as I live," I said.

"How about drinking to peace, then?"

I looked thoughtfully into the distance. "Let's drink to the fallen."

I looked back at Ziggy, and he too quickly became serious. "To the fallen." We smiled sadly at each other; we knew what each of us meant.

"Now let's drink next to the future," Ziggy said then. "To the Jewish homeland."

"It's true then? What they are saying?"

Ziggy brightened as we clinked glasses. "Yes, a future for the Jews in Eretz Israel. Although the British are not making it easy." He dropped his voice and whispered, "I don't want to insult our British hosts here, but Britain will have to be pushed into granting the Jews what we have earned and paid with our lives for."

I had to smile a little, thinking of Mihail and Jonah. I decided that I would keep some of my views to myself. "If Israel is possible, then anything is possible."

"So . . ." Ziggy said, "that means I might have a future, too? With you, I mean?"

I smiled wider as I daintily sipped at my drink. I liked him. The nurses teased and nudged us both, laughing. Everybody was eager to get their lives back after the horrors of the war.

"Anything and everything is possible!" We all shouted and raised our glasses.

"To the possibilities!" I smiled, too, but moments later, suddenly and unexpectedly, I felt the exuberance draining from me like a sponge that was saturated. I could stand only so much joy without some terrible moment intruding into my consciousness. The vivid memories lurked in the back of my mind like predators, watching for a moment of vulnerability, of carefree high spirits before pouncing.

Suddenly I craved my loneliness and isolation back again. It felt like a comfortable old garment. Loneliness never made promises and never disappointed.

But I fought off the depression with the help of a few more drinks. I brought Ziggy home with me that night, and we made love hungrily and joyously. I got out my jug of vodka and despite Philippa's well-intentioned

schooling, we passed it back and forth and got uproari-
ously crazy until we saw the dawn brightening the sky. By
then I had promised to marry him. We fell asleep at last
in each other's arms.

But once again, the horrors of the war were only waiting for me to drop my guard.

Sleep with No Rest

I RUN FOR MY LIFE, all hope gone, all caution cast aside. I am in an autumn forest, and although I recognize nothing around me, somehow I know I am near Yedinitz, my home village in Romania. Even as I flee, I am stunned at the beauty of this land: the sky a deep and tender blue, the sun radiant and pure, the coppers and russets and golds of the beeches and poplars brilliant. Too brilliant. And this was how I realized, even in my dream, that this was not real.

Still, I was in no hurry to awaken. I was warmly dressed, though a brisk wind cooled my face, and the earth gave off a mulchy aroma as my feet churned the thick, damp carpet of dead leaves. But now, my breath began to come in harsh, raw gasps; my shoes started skidding uselessly on the slick footing. I could not gain enough traction to run; and I sensed that the Iron Guard was very close.

I didn't dare pause; and only then did I notice that I was clutching the hand of Jacob, my little brother. His delicate fingers were wrapped tightly around mine. I was careful not to squeeze too hard; his fingers were for his music. And sure enough, his precious violin case swung and swayed from his right hand, hitting him about the knees and legs as he ran.

Branches caught and pulled at my gray woolen coat. Jacob stumbled, and I yanked him to his feet and dragged him when his legs went out from under him. A dank, smoky odor filled my nostrils. And just then I saw it, the train, stopped at a tiny station. We were in time! We had made it. But where were the tickets? Why, here they were clutched in my other hand; how did I not notice them? As we drew near, the train steamed and tooted comfortingly. It even emitted a gasp of relief.

"We are safe, little brother," I murmured, looking down on the top of Jacob's head, for I could not see his face. We raced into the station clearing, and how massive the train was up close, how solid and black it was; how grimy and gritty the dark, steamy smoke that surrounded it. I was smiling with joy—but what if it pulled out before we could board?

My knees were collapsing; I found a car with the door open and scrambled up the metal steps hauling Jacob after me just in time. We were safe. "Wait!" I laughed to my brother, already running down the aisle, holding his violin case in front of him with both hands.

I nearly lost my balance as the train lurched into motion and began to pull away slowly, gathering speed. I tried to urge it forward, relief flooding into me, I couldn't believe my good fortune. Faster, faster it went. I looked around for a seat. "Jacob!" I called. "Come back! We must take our seats." The people in the car turned to look at me. "It's my little brother!" I laughed to the audience. "He's too quick! I cannot hold him."

But now, rather than gaining momentum, the train

suddenly began to slow. Why should this be? And then I heard it, faint at first but growing louder as the cry passed from car to car: "Jews! There are Jews aboard. They have to be found!" I tried to appear as puzzled as I could manage, looking around for the "Jews" just like the others. In my dread, I wondered if Jacob looked too Jewish—would they guess? Would he give us away? And where was he? My heart nearly stopped: Had they caught him already?

Outside, I saw the dreaded green shirts of the Iron Guard; they were close enough to look in through the windows, shouting to one another. On their uniforms, I saw an incomprehensible patch here, a flag there, with its bizarre black grid. And oddly, I saw no faces—only the backs of their necks with their brutally barbered pig-bristle hairlines. Their hair was shaved short around the head but the crown hair was left longer so that it flopped down over the shaved area. The hairstyle was popular with Hitler's soldiers, and so the Iron Guard bullies aped their Nazi overlords. I saw their fingers, blunt, short, and cruel, clutching their guns.

Now my heart sank. I knew that we were caught; that the outcry was about us, and that Jacob and I were going to die. Perhaps within moments our blood would be running red among the bright leaves and young trees outside.

But no, this was impossible! Jacob was already dead, I recalled. And I wanted to cry out and explain. This could not be happening; it made no sense. Was I dead, too, then? My voice was gone. I opened my mouth and no sound came out, not even a breath. I struggled mightily to scream as the soldiers turned to look at me.

I opened my eyes. My room was cool, quiet, and dim;

familiar shapes and silhouettes of shabby furniture were barely visible in the early dawn. I must have been sleeping only a few minutes. Beside me, Ziggy, my new lover and soon to be husband, slept silently, his broad, muscular back turned to me. I had managed not to wake him, despite my thrashing and struggling. I saw with relief that I had not cried out; my pounding heart did not give me away. My nightmare was safe.

Zig sighed in his sleep: who knew what his own dreams were—of his own boyhood that he told me about during the Depression in the poor Jewish ghetto of North Minneapolis, getting pummeled in Golden Gloves boxing matches with the other boys, children of struggling immigrants; rising at 4:00 A.M. to deliver newspapers in twenty-below-zero weather. Or perhaps he is in the cockpit of his B-24 Liberator, rattling and bouncing amid the flak, watching fellow pilots crash in flames. Or looking down to see the firestorms that their bombs have ignited in the German cities. Ziggy had plenty of fuel himself for nightmares, and I inwardly vowed to help him overcome his own horrors.

But suddenly—traitorously—I thought of the boy-man Mihail and our sensual afternoons on the count's estate, in the groom's quarters. Even now, the memory of him made my body tense and soften at the same time, as if he were indeed here with me, the memory so sweet that it drew me, captured me.

Later that morning, working in the nursing ward with my ferocious hangover, I felt bold enough to revisit the forest of my dream. What was that place? Did I live another life? I cannot remember anything like my dream ever happening to me. I never fled the Iron Guard with Jacob.

He was dead many weeks before we left Yedinitz. So the dream was a complete artifact of my subconscious. And why did I feel nostalgia during my walk through the forest? Nostalgia for Romania? How could that be? The accursed place that I was so grateful to have left that I gave thanks every conscious moment.

According to the latest physics, the past could never return or trade places with the future. I was safe here in the present, and the future welcomed me. Ziggy's postwar plans were to become a housing contractor amid the boom already gathering momentum in America. He told me that we would live in Minneapolis, "The City of Ten Thousand Lakes," and he described these little sapphires in the middle of a bustling, prosperous town untouched by warfare, by tanks and marching soldiers and artillery, by bombs and fire. He would build me a home on a beach beside this fresh, clear water, he promised.

Water. How thirsty we were, I recall now, on the Transnistria Death March. They would not let us drink. We came to the Dniester River after marching for countless miles. How we craved a sip of water; and we had only to reach down. It was flowing cold and fresh about our feet.

And why didn't we? Because anybody who tried to drink, who paused for even a moment, was shot dead. The river became their grave. As we lurched up the hill with our bleeding feet, the guards seemed to relent. Those who had reached the top, they told us, would be allowed to descend again and drink. How we stampeded for that abundant water. Even the elderly, the half dead, ran. And what do you think? There was no end to the evil of the Romanian guards. The moment we reached the shore, they raised their guns—it had all been a game. A prank. Those who stepped into the water or cupped their hands or bent to drink were shot. But by then, I did not care anymore. I threw myself into the torrent and drank beside the body of a dead man. I filled my mouth with the river water, awaiting the fatal bullet, drinking with my last breath.

I told Ziggy only a portion of the outrages I suffered. As far as he was concerned, he told me, he was my first lover, and I was grateful that he was able to feel that way. But the other men I had known have all left their marks on me and shaped who I was, for better—and for worse. So it was with all people, men and women alike. We all carried our experiences with us all our lives, and it was best to accept them and not judge or condemn ourselves, but take from them what could make us stronger and more compassionate to others in their own struggles.

Epilogue

PHILIPPA EMIGRATED to Australia after the war and married a sheep farmer. This sophisticated daughter of a British aristocrat and mistress of a Romanian count now works shearing sheep and caring for lambs, and she is, as she confesses, "always pregnant."

Ziggy and I have just arrived in America, newlyweds fresh from a hasty ceremony in a drafty, tiny London office. We are meeting his brother Mel and wife Madelynne for cocktails and dinner at a restaurant called the Waikiki Room in downtown Minneapolis. It's wintertime, and our feet crunch on the crisp snow outside, which sparkles like diamonds under the streetlights shining down on the neatly cleared sidewalk. I think of the winters during the war when I would spend days and weeks slogging in frozen mud without ever getting warm, and I hug Ziggy's latest gift around my shoulders: a lush fox stole.

Beneath it, I am wearing a spaghetti strap dress of royal blue satin and *peau de soie*. I love the dress, though I know that Mama would have done something far more stunning with this costly fabric. But I look pretty tonight, and Ziggy loves to see me dressed up.

The waistline is very snug, as is the style these days,

and Ziggy is amazed at my twenty-four-inch waist. He takes simple pride in showing off his young wife, and why not? He cannot help feeling as he does. He considers me a sort of prize, a possession.

"You survived the war because you were so pretty," he once said to me. "You were lucky." I thought of Priva, with her silky auburn hair and blue eyes. Her good looks had only helped seal her fate.

"Ziggy, my looks could as easily have gotten me killed as saved me."

"I was only trying to give you a compliment."

"I know," I say, realizing that some memories and thoughts I would just have to keep to myself.

We are welcomed into the restaurant with fresh flower leis presented by girls in whispering, swinging grass skirts to the accompaniment of Hawaiian hula music. I cannot believe the ingenuity of Americans in creating a Polynesian resort in the middle of a near-Arctic winter here in Minnesota. Outside, it will dip below zero tonight—but within here the air is balmy and moist. Great effort has been expended to create a total escape to a different world. We are surrounded by exotic ferns and coral and bamboo; fantastic reed boats hang on the walls, and flowers burst forth wherever the eye lands. The air smells of frangipani, and I am given a huge, perfect gardenia to wear in my hair.

I tuck it behind my ear. I have let my hair grow long again after cropping it short during the war. Once when I was starving in Transnistria it had started to fall out, but under the major's nurturing care and nutritious food, it had grown back glossy and thick.

The major had loved my hair. He had loved me, in his

brutal, barbaric, nihilistic way. I cannot explain to anyone that I even miss him sometimes, with his hard edge and uncompromisingly honest attitude toward the war. I even miss the imitations he would do of the German big shots and the jokes he would tell me, just to make me smile. How could I feel affection for the man who exploited me so shamelessly? And yet he had saved my life and treated me as one of his family, a family which was, of course, dead. All of our families were dead, and so we had had to find others to bond with. I certainly can't confide all of these feelings to Ziggy, and I keep many memories to myself.

I have managed to keep all of my teeth, too, despite the constant violence that had been wrought on me by soldiers during the Transnistrian march. Ziggy had a dentist whiten and polish my teeth because, after all, I represent him and his family, so I must look my best.

I have discovered that Ziggy's mother, Rose, thinks that I am too "foreign" for him, although she herself is the daughter of Lithuanian Jews who emigrated in 1915 and so missed the Holocaust, which killed nearly all the Jews in her city of Vilna.

I want to scream at her, "How can you even think this way when six million of us are dead?" She has never so much as missed a single meal during her entire life, even during the war. I could tell her stories to put her in her place, but I keep silent.

"Mom thinks you have no sense of humor," Ziggy told me once. "It wouldn't hurt you to loosen up a little when she's around. Mom's not such a bad type. In fact you're a lot alike."

"Please don't ever say that."

"I understand she's a little tough on you. That's because I'm her favorite."

Rose also doesn't understand why my family didn't leave Romania before the Nazis invaded. I had made the mistake of telling her that I could have left my family and escaped with the count and countess. "Why didn't you go?" she exclaimed. "Your parents should have forced you to go."

"They tried," I said. "They begged me."

So she blames Mama and Papa for keeping me from escaping. "I would have *forced* you to go with the countess," Rose said with smug certainty. I felt a sudden, powerful urge to slap her face, but years of self-discipline held my anger in, and I only turned away. I gave up trying to explain what it was like on that terrible morning.

"Try to put up with her," Ziggy tells me afterward. "She just doesn't understand, but she means well."

"I don't think she means well at all," I reply to him. "I think . . ." But I stop myself. I cannot risk alienating my husband.

Now the scent of the gardenia nearly makes me dizzy. I recall the flowers in our yard in Yedinitz and how Philippa used to sometimes twine forget-me-nots into her hair. I am lost in thought while the world washes around me, as if I am actually on an island in this imaginary Pacific Ocean.

Our drinks arrive, and I gratefully sip away at an enormous hollowed-out pineapple, filled with rum and exotic liqueurs, along with cherries and melon all combined into a heady concoction. I feel a relaxing and enjoyable flush from the drink and grow warm, putting my new fox stole beside me.

A photographer arrives and positions himself to snap a picture of our whole table. After the flash, my eye falls on the stole. Then, I look more closely at it. The foxes, who are all biting one another's tails, seem to be staring at me. It is as if they recognize me from the forests of Bessarabia. "We know you," they cry out silently. "After all that's happened, you end up eating Polynesian shrimp and drinking Mai Tais. But we won't let you forget us."

I turn the fox stole over so that I cannot see their dead, polished eyes. I drink my drink quickly and order another as Ziggy lights two cigarettes and passes one to me. Soon we are laughing and toasting one another. The food is amazingly delicious. I can have anything I want on the menu. If I wanted to order a second dinner Ziggy would not hesitate. I cannot even pronounce the name of the elegant entrée I am eating. . . .

Mel and Madelynne insist that we spend the night in their new split-level home. The guest bedroom is almost as large as my home's entire lower story in Yedinitz. Ziggy and I arrive still giddy from our Mai Tais, and we fall into bed laughing and eager to make love, then drowse off to sleep.

I am lost in a dense and menacing forest; something is stalking me. I cannot see it, but I know it is there. Close to the misty ground, the speed and momentum of my pursuer grow. Suddenly, growling and thrashing erupt as several unseen predators pounce on something. They have found food and are battling fiercely over it.

I awaken in terror with a gasp, and Ziggy quickly sits up.

"Daniela? What is it? What's wrong?"

I am not entirely awake. I keep trying to pull myself

from my unconsciousness, but the dream doesn't want to let me go. It is trying to hold me hostage in its reality.

I see the eyes of the foxes.

"They're eating him! The foxes!" A tidal wave of horror washes over me. I gasp and try to hold in the scream that rises inside me.

Ziggy, his face creased with concern, reaches out and takes me in his arms. As he rocks me, I become fully conscious at last. I look around and see with relief the plush, comfortable furniture in the elegant bedroom. I see Ziggy holding me as he rocks me. I feel the comforting spun cotton of the sheets and his warmth beneath them.

"Daniela, hush," he whispers in my ear. Of course, I must get control of myself. I begin to cry but softly as my terror diminishes.

"I cannot stand to live another minute with what I see in my mind!"

"Shhh. It's over. Daniela."

"It will never be over."

"They are at peace now. Every one of them."

"If only it were so!"

Gradually, I stop shuddering and sobbing. Holding me, Ziggy looks grimly into the dark.

"Oh God, why did you want to marry me? I am damaged goods."

He continues to rock me soothingly. "Because I loved you the moment I saw you."

"You loved my . . . my body." I pull back and look at him chidingly, eyes brimming with tears.

"So? Is that a crime? I saw this great-looking girl who happened to be Jewish. . . . You think I'm sorry?"

"You should be. You're getting a bad bargain."

Ziggy gives me a pill, which soon softens and covers over my ragged emotions. As I am falling asleep, I see him rise and take the fox stole from the bureau where I had tossed it when we came in.

I see him put on his shoes and overcoat and let himself out of the house, carrying the stole. I rise and peek from the window that looks out on the yard as Ziggy makes his way to the trash can. He opens it and throws the stole in. The dead foxes seem to gaze up at him chidingly. He pauses, but only for a moment, then he shakes his head and closes the lid on them. He turns and walks back inside, a lonely figure in the moonlight, as a wave of drowsiness washes over me, carrying me toward a place where the war cannot reach me. I snuggle into Ziggy's arms and let his love bear me away into the healing deep.

"In the grey tumult of these after years,
  Oft silence falls; the incessant wranglers part;
  And less-than-echoes of remembered tears
  Hush all the loud confusion of the heart . . ."
                                        —Rupert Brooke

About the Author

Linda Boroff's writing appears in *McSweeney's*, *All the Sins*, *The Write Launch*, *Parhelion*, *Close to the Bone*, *Crack the Spine*, *Writing Disorder*, *The Piltdown Review*, *The Lowestoft Chronicle*, *Eclectica*, *5:21 Magazine*, *Thoughtful Dog*, *The Satirist*, *Fleas on the Dog*, *Hollywood Dementia*, *Sundress*, *In Posse Review*, *Adelaide Magazine*, *Word Riot*, *Ducts*, *Blunderbuss*, *Storyglossia*, *The Furious Gazelle*, *The Pedestal Magazine*, *Eyeshot*, *JONAH Magazine*, *The Boiler*, *Bound Off*, *Black Denim Lit*, *Stirring*, *Drunk Monkeys*, and *Fictive Dream*.

Linda's suspense novella, *The Remnant*, was published in June 2020. A collection of linked short stories, *All I Can Take of You*, was published in August 2020 by Adelaide Press. Her latest novel, *Twisted Fate*, is coming in 2022 from Champagne Book Group. She was nominated in 2021 and 2016 for a Pushcart Prize in fiction. A short story is currently under option to director Brad Furman and Sony. Linda Boroff also wrote the feature film, *Murder in Fashion*. She graduated from UC Berkeley with a degree in English and currently lives and works in Silicon Valley.